Boca Raton Public Library, Boca Raton, FL

MyReportLinks.com Books, an imprint of Enslow Publishers, Inc. MyReportLinks® is a registered trademark of Enslow Publishers, Inc.

Copyright © 2008 by Enslow Publishers, Inc.

All rights reserved.

No part of this book may be reproduced by any means without the written permission of the publisher.

Library of Congress Cataloging-in-Publication Data

Aretha, David.
  Steel tough—the Pittsburgh Steelers / David Aretha. — 1st ed.
    p. cm. — (Sensational sports teams)
  Includes bibliographical references and index.
  ISBN-13: 978-1-59845-047-7
  ISBN-10: 1-59845-047-6
  1. Pittsburgh Steelers (Football team)—History—Juvenile literature. I. Title.
  GV956.P57A74 2008
  796.332'640974886—dc22
                                        2006025414

Printed in the United States of America

10 9 8 7 6 5 4 3 2 1

To Our Readers:
Through the purchase of this book, you and your library gain access to the Report Links that specifically back up this book.
The Publisher will provide access to the Report Links that back up this book and will keep these Report Links up to date on **www.myreportlinks.com** for five years from the book's first publication date.
We have done our best to make sure all Internet addresses in this book were active and appropriate when we went to press. However, the author and the Publisher have no control over, and assume no liability for, the material available on those Internet sites or on other Web sites they may link to.
The usage of the MyReportLinks.com Books Web site is subject to the terms and conditions stated on the Usage Policy Statement on **www.myreportlinks.com**.
A password may be required to access the Report Links that back up this book. The password is found on the bottom of page 4 of this book.
Any comments or suggestions can be sent by e-mail to comments@myreportlinks.com or to the address on the back cover.

Photo Credits: American Iron and Steel Institute, p. 57; AP/Wide World Photos, pp. 1, 3, 6, 11, 14, 20, 24, 31, 38–39, 42, 48, 54, 61, 64, 66, 70, 73, 78, 86, 88, 91, 95, 97, 99, 101, 103, 105, 107, 109, 112; CBC/Radio Canada, p. 92; ESPN Internet Ventures, p. 45; FansEdge, Inc., p. 59; John Henry Johnson c/o CMG Worldwide, p. 21; MMVI Tank Productions, p. 35; MyReportLinks.com Books, p. 4; NFL Enterprises, LLC, pp. 9, 43, 52, 77; PG Publishing Co., pp. 27, 55, 68; *Pittsburgh Post Gazette*, p. 46; Pittsburgh Steelers, pp. 40, 87; Professional Football Researchers Association, p. 19; Pro Football Hall of Fame, pp. 63, 94; Shutterstock.com, p. 1; Stadiums of the NFL, p. 81; Steelers Fever, p. 83; The Jerome Bettis Bus Stops Here Foundation, p. 111; The Museum of Broadcast Communications, p. 85; The Official Lynn Swann Web Site, p. 29; The Washington Post Company, p. 33; The White House, p. 12; Time Inc., p. 72; 2005 Life Inc., p. 75; UK Black & Gold, p. 22; Unitas Management Corporation, p. 17.

Cover Photo: AP/Wide World Photos; Shutterstock.com (Field background)

Cover Description: Ben Roethlisberger, Steelers quarterback.

Contents

About MyReportLinks.com Books 4
Steelers Facts 5
1 Riding "The Bus" to the
   Super Bowl 7
2 Four Decades of Futility 15
3 Stainless Steel Trophies 25
4 The Power of Cowher 49
5 The Masterminds 67
6 Welcome to Heinz Field 79
7 The Heroes 89
   Report Links 114
   Career Stats 116
   Glossary 118
   Chapter Notes 120
   Further Reading 125
   Index 126

About MyReportLinks.com Books

MyReportLinks.com Books
Great Books, Great Links, Great for Research!

The Internet sites featured in this book can save you hours of research time. These Internet sites—we call them **"Report Links"**—are constantly changing, but we keep them up to date on our Web site.

When you see this "Approved Web Site" logo, you will know that we are directing you to a great Internet site that will help you with your research.

Give it a try! Type http://www.myreportlinks.com into your browser, click on the series title and enter the password, then click on the book title, and scroll down to the Report Links listed for this book.

The Report Links will bring you to great source documents, photographs, and illustrations. MyReportLinks.com Books save you time, feature Report Links that are kept up to date, and make report writing easier than ever! A complete listing of the Report Links can be found on pages 114–115 at the back of the book.

Please see "To Our Readers" on the copyright page for important information about this book, the MyReportLinks.com Web site, and the Report Links that back up this book.

Please enter **PSF1958** if asked for a password.

Steelers Facts

- First Season: 1933 (known as the Pittsburgh Pirates until 1941)
- Super Bowl Champions: IX (1975); X (1976); XIII (1979); XIV (1980); XL (2006).

HOME FIELD	
1933–57	Forbes Field
1958–63	Forbes Field and Pitt Stadium
1964–69	Pitt Stadium
1970–2000	Three Rivers Stadium
2001–Present	Heinz Field

HALL OF FAMERS	POSITION	SEASONS WITH STEELERS
Bert Bell	Co-owner	1941–46
Mel Blount	Cornerback	1970–83
Terry Bradshaw	Quarterback	1970–83
Bill Dudley	Running Back	1942, 1945–46
Joe Greene	Defensive Tackle	1969–81
Jack Ham	Linebacker	1971–82
Franco Harris	Running Back	1972–83
John Henry Johnson	Running Back	1960–65
Walt Kiesling	Guard	1937–39
Walt Kiesling	Head Coach	1939–44, 1954–56
Jack Lambert	Linebacker	1974–84
Bobby Layne	Quarterback	1958–62
Johnny "Blood" McNally	Running Back	1934, 1937–39
Chuck Noll	Head Coach	1969–91
Art Rooney	Owner	1933–88
Dan Rooney	Owner	1955–present
John Stallworth	Wide Receiver	1974–87
Ernie Stautner	Defensive Tackle	1950–63
Lynn Swann	Wide Receiver	1974–82
Mike Webster	Center	1974–88

▲ Steelers running back Jerome Bettis holds the Super Bowl trophy high in the air after Super Bowl XL.

Riding "The Bus" to the Super Bowl

1

As he stood in the tunnel at Detroit's Ford Field, a million thoughts must have raced through the mind of Jerome Bettis. For ten of his thirteen NFL seasons, the 255-pound running back had busted tackles for the Pittsburgh Steelers. "The Bus" had amassed 13,662 yards, fifth most in NFL history. But, oh, the punishment he had endured: three major knee surgeries, scoped ankles, and a groin muscle ripped off the bone. The list of ailments included torn muscles and ligaments, broken ribs, numerous concussions, and a rearranged nose. At age thirty-three, Bettis went through agony just climbing a set of stairs. Yet here he was in February 2006, about to play in his very first Super Bowl.

Bettis had been determined to retire a year earlier, but a guilt-ridden teammate helped change his mind. During the 2004 season, the Steelers had finished 15–1 thanks largely to the team's rookie quarterback—Ben Roethlisberger. But Pittsburgh lost the AFC Championship Game to New England. Roethlisberger, who threw 3 interceptions, felt responsible. The young QB promised Bettis that if Bettis came back for one more season, he would quarterback the team to the Super Bowl. Bettis knew that the Super Bowl would be in Detroit, his beloved home city. "The last thing I wanted to see was [the Steelers] in my hometown without me," Bettis said. "I couldn't live with that."[1] So he returned for one more season of agony, dreaming of glory.

In December, Roethlisberger had little hope of fulfilling his promise. The Steelers were 7–5 and were long shots to make the playoffs in the talent-rich AFC. Stunningly, they defeated the Chicago Bears, who had won eight straight games, then blew away Minnesota and Cleveland. In the season finale, Pittsburgh beat Detroit 35–21 on the strength of Bettis's 3 touchdowns. As he left the game, Steelers fans showered him with a standing ovation.

At 11–5, the Steelers made the playoffs as a No. 6 seed. This meant that to reach the Super Bowl, they would have to win three playoff games—all of which would be on the road. Bettis scored to help Pittsburgh win its first postseason game at Cincinnati, 31–17. But Bettis almost blew

Riding "The Bus" to the Super Bowl

the game the next week at Indianapolis. With 1:20 remaining and Pittsburgh leading 21–18, The Bus fumbled on the Colts' 2-yard line. Indy's Nick Harper almost returned it the other way for a touchdown, but he was tripped up by Roethlisberger. The Colts missed a field goal attempt, keeping Roethlisberger's promise alive.

Prior to the AFC Championship Game at Denver, Bettis delivered a stirring pep talk to his teammates. "Just get me to Detroit," he pleaded.[2] They did, winning 34–17. After the game, Bettis found his parents in the crowd and said, "We're going home."[3]

Over the next two weeks, Bettis was the most celebrated man in America. Teammates praised

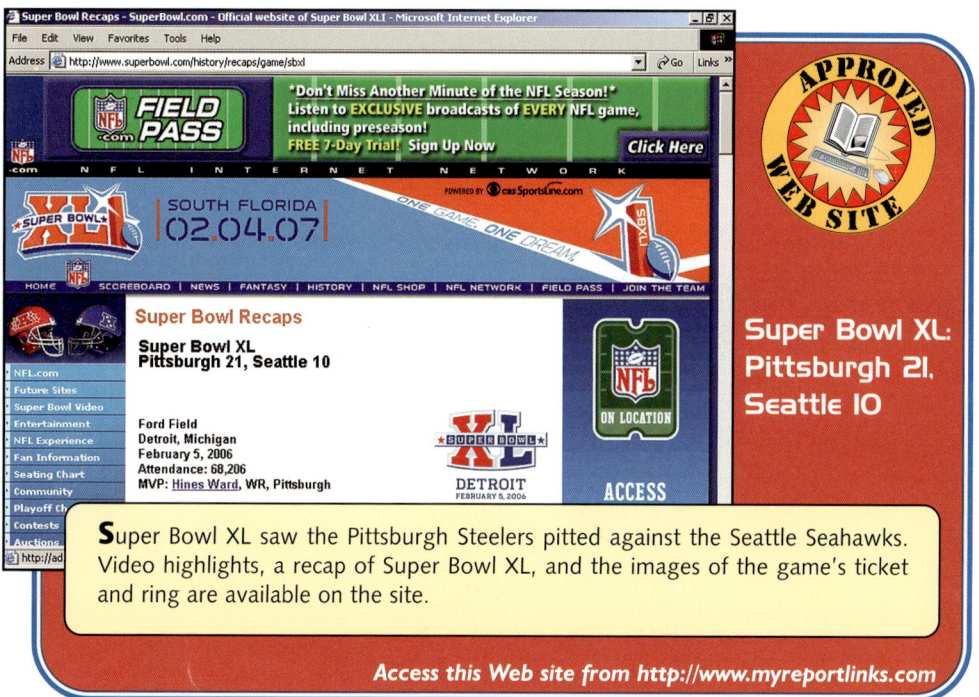

Super Bowl XL: Pittsburgh 21, Seattle 10

Super Bowl XL saw the Pittsburgh Steelers pitted against the Seattle Seahawks. Video highlights, a recap of Super Bowl XL, and the images of the game's ticket and ring are available on the site.

Access this Web site from http://www.myreportlinks.com

his work ethic and inspirational leadership. "He's touched every player in that locker room in some form," said Steelers receiver Hines Ward.[4] Meanwhile, "Jerome Bettis Week" was declared in Detroit. Bettis had donated tens of thousands of dollars to his former Detroit high school, and he had invested money to revitalize downtown. He once was named NFL Man of the Year for his work with underprivileged children and asthma patients.

"Jerome is a shining example of what a kid with a dream from Detroit can accomplish with hard work and determination," said Detroit Mayor Kwame Kilpatrick.[5] Added Carol Tate, Bettis's high school math teacher, "When I watch his games, when I see him on TV, I can't help but get a little emotional."[6]

Roethlisberger, meanwhile, could not handle another stirring speech by Bettis. "I'm going to tell him not to say too much [before the Super Bowl], because I don't want to start getting teary-eyed," Roethlisberger said. "We don't want a bunch of guys crying coming out of the locker room."[7]

But prior to the big game, linebacker Joey Porter asked Bettis to be the first player out of the tunnel—to lead the Steelers onto the field. Bettis called it an unforgettable moment. Sixty-eight thousand fans, most of whom were Steelers faithful, roared for their hero and waved their "Terrible Towels."

▲ *Shaun Alexander of the Seahawks is wrapped up by Steelers linebacker Joey Porter during the fourth quarter of Super Bowl XL.*

Bettis had waited thirteen years for this day, but Steelers fans were even hungrier for a title. Their team had won four Super Bowl rings in the 1970s, but the people of Pittsburgh still longed for "One for the Thumb." A whole nation tuned in with keen interest to see the Steelers take on the offensively explosive Seattle Seahawks. The game would be seen in 45.85 million American homes—a number surpassed only by the series finale of *M*A*S*H* in 1983.

Detroit put on an extraordinary show. Stevie Wonder, Aaron Neville, and Aretha Franklin sang before the game, and the Rolling Stones performed at halftime. More than thirty former Super Bowl MVPs were honored in a pregame ceremony.

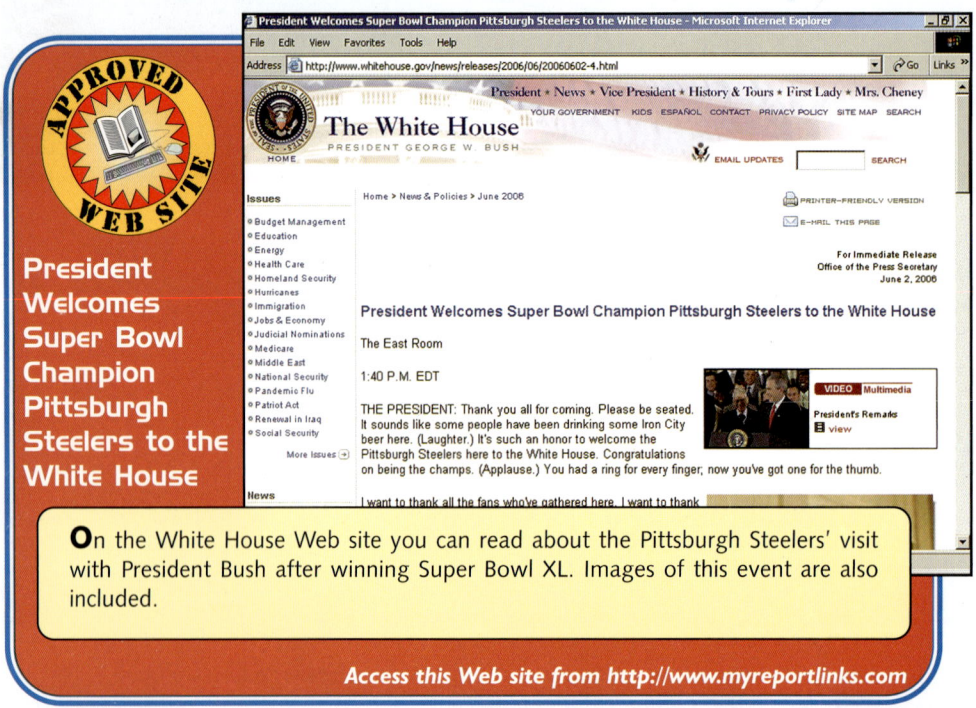

President Welcomes Super Bowl Champion Pittsburgh Steelers to the White House

On the White House Web site you can read about the Pittsburgh Steelers' visit with President Bush after winning Super Bowl XL. Images of this event are also included.

Access this Web site from http://www.myreportlinks.com

Riding "The Bus" to the Super Bowl

This exciting game itself featured three of the most spectacular touchdown plays in Super Bowl history (see Chapter 4).

With the Steelers leading 21–10 in the fourth quarter, Roethlisberger gave it to The Bus play after play. Seven times he lugged the pigskin, as Pittsburgh kept moving the chains. By the time the Seahawks finally got the ball back, with 1:51 left and no time-outs remaining, their fate was sealed. Pittsburgh prevailed 21–10, becoming the first NFL team ever to win four postseason road games en route to the title.

Usually, players dump a tub of Gatorade on their coach's head, but this team saved the honor for Bettis. "It was Jerome's day," said Porter. "It was his time to shine in his hometown."[8] Said Bettis himself: "It's totally, totally a blessing. I'm probably the luckiest football player who ever played."[9]

Amid the on-field celebration, Bettis addressed the crowd of Detroiters and Steelers fans—and a worldwide television audience. In grand style, he definitively announced his retirement. "[There's] always a time when you have to call it quits," he said. "I played to win a championship, and now I'm a champion. The Bus's last stop is here in Detroit."[10]

This 1946 image shows many of the early owners of NFL franchises. Art Rooney is standing second from the right.

Four Decades of Futility

In 1982, eighty-one-year-old Steelers owner Art Rooney reflected on the team he had built from scratch. From his office desk drawer, he pulled out old ledgers, including one from 1933. "I found these when we moved here," Rooney said. "I don't think anybody around here is interested in them, but they bring back a lot of memories for me."[1]

Rooney, known for his kindness, sportsmanship, and ever-present cigar, was the man who brought NFL football to Pittsburgh. It all started back in the late 1920s. Rooney ran a strong semi-pro team known as the Hope-Harveys, comprised of coal miners and steelworkers. The club was good enough to compete in the NFL, but a Pennsylvania law banned professional football games on Sunday. When that law was repealed in 1933, Rooney signed a $2,500 check and started an NFL franchise. He called the team the

Pittsburgh Pirates, the same name as the city's major-league baseball team.

⊙ Starting Out

On September 20, 1933, the later-renamed Steelers played their first NFL game. But the thirteen thousand fans at Forbes Field (the baseball Pirates' ballpark) had only a safety to cheer for. The New York Giants won 23–2, in a game that set the tone for the rest of the decade. Through 1940, Rooney's football Pirates went a combined 24–62–5. Worse, the Great Depression of the 1930s crippled attendance revenue. Recalled Rooney, "The biggest thrill wasn't in winning on Sunday but in meeting the payroll on Monday."[2]

The Pirates lost $100,000 during the 1930s, yet their owner refused to give up on his team. Fortunately for Rooney, he caught a lucky break at the racetrack in 1936. One Saturday, he turned $300 into $21,000 in winnings. Even luckier on Monday, he upped his take to $256,000!

The Pirates were renamed the Steelers prior to the 1940 season. After going 2–7–2 that year, Rooney sold the team for $160,000. Several months later, he bought it back.

World War II took a heavy toll on the NFL rosters, as most able-bodied men joined the service. In 1943, the Steelers and Philadelphia Eagles merged to form the Phil-Pitt Eagles and were

Four Decades of Futility

known as the Steagles. The team went 5–4–1. The following season, Pittsburgh joined with the Chicago Cardinals to become the "Card-Pitts." This motley crew was so bad (they lost every game that season) that fans called them the "Carpets" because opponents walked all over them.

In 1947, esteemed head coach Jock Sutherland led Pittsburgh to an 8–4 record and its first-ever playoff game. Fans who envisioned a string of championships were sadly mistaken. The Steelers lost that postseason game to Philadelphia, 21–0. The following spring, Sutherland died of a brain

The official Web site of **Johnny Unitas.** Quarterback Johnny Unitas was drafted by the Pittsburgh Steelers but never played for the team. He went on to have a superstar career with teams such as the Baltimore Colts.

tumor. Pittsburgh would not make the playoffs again for another twenty-five years.

S.O.S.

From 1948 through 1956, the Steelers played 12 games each season but never won more than six of them. The front office doomed the team with especially bad decisions. The Steelers drafted quarterback Johnny Unitas in 1955, then cut him because coach Walt Kiesling did not think he was smart enough. Unitas went on to become one of the greatest quarterbacks of all time. In 1957, Pittsburgh could have selected running back Jim Brown with the fifth pick in the draft. They passed. Brown became, in many people's minds, the best player in NFL history.

In 1957, Rooney hired his first big-name NFL coach. Ray "Buddy" Parker had won two NFL championships with the Detroit Lions. From 1957 through 1964, Parker led Pittsburgh to a 51–47–6 overall record. Bobby Layne, who had led Detroit to greatness, quarterbacked the Steelers for five seasons. John Henry Johnson rushed for more than a thousand yards in 1962 and 1964. Yet Parker could not get Pittsburgh into the playoffs, and he left in a huff shortly before the 1965 season.

Linebacker Andy Russell recalled how the Steelers deteriorated in the mid-1960s. "Guys like

Four Decades of Futility

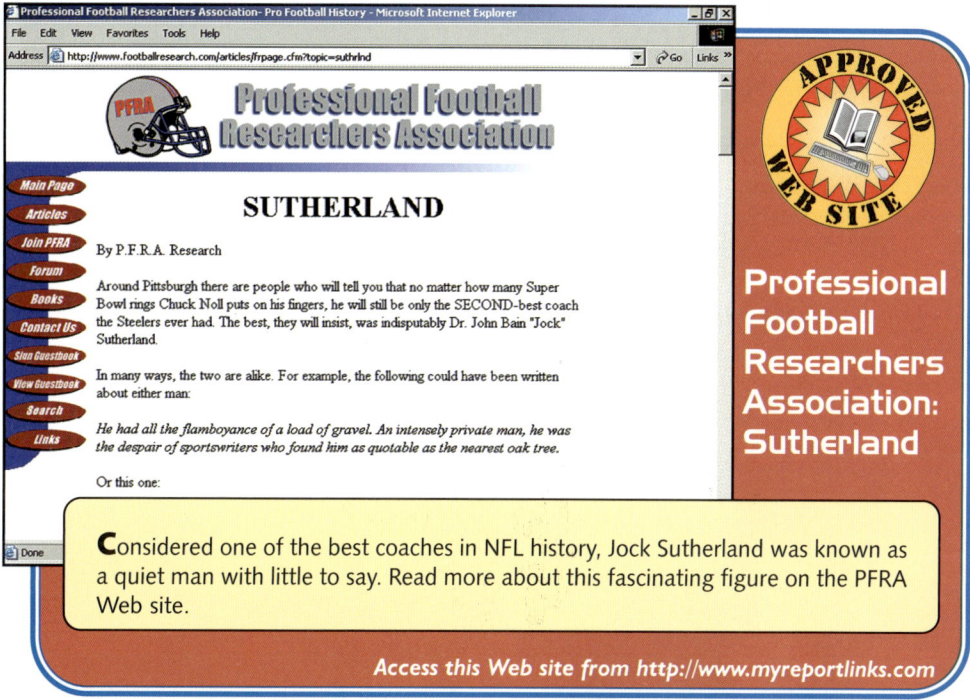

Professional Football Researchers Association: Sutherland

Considered one of the best coaches in NFL history, Jock Sutherland was known as a quiet man with little to say. Read more about this fascinating figure on the PFRA Web site.

Access this Web site from http://www.myreportlinks.com

[All-Pro defensive lineman] Ernie Stautner, all the old players that were around in '63, were gone," he said. "And they had not done a very good job of drafting, so there wasn't much talent, and we struggled hugely for the next couple of years."[3]

From 1965 through 1968, the Steelers posted sorrowful records of 2–12, 5–8–1, 4–9–1, and 2–11–1. At home games, fans displayed signs that read "S.O.S." In the Navy, that means "save our ship" because it is sinking. In Pittsburgh, it stood for "Same Old Steelers." Art Rooney, as well as his sons, Dan and Art, Jr., who helped him run the team, knew the team needed a savior. They would find him in Baltimore, Maryland.

▲ *Steelers head coach Chuck Noll instructs his team.*

Four Decades of Futility

➲ Noll to the Rescue

After the 1968 season, the Steelers went shopping for a new head coach. Dan Rooney wanted to hire someone who knew how to win in the NFL, so he contacted Baltimore Colts head coach Don Shula. Shula recommended one of his assistants, thirty-seven-year-old Chuck Noll. Few NFL fans knew about the quiet, unassuming coach. However, he had helped Cleveland to NFL championships as a player in the 1950s. In 1968, he had contributed to Baltimore's 13–1 record. He was a brilliant student of the game, and he knew how to win.

During his NFL years, Johnson played for three teams: the San Francisco 49ers, the Detroit Lions, and the Pittsburgh Steelers. He was also considered one of the best runners in the game. Learn more about him at this **John Henry Johnson** Web page.

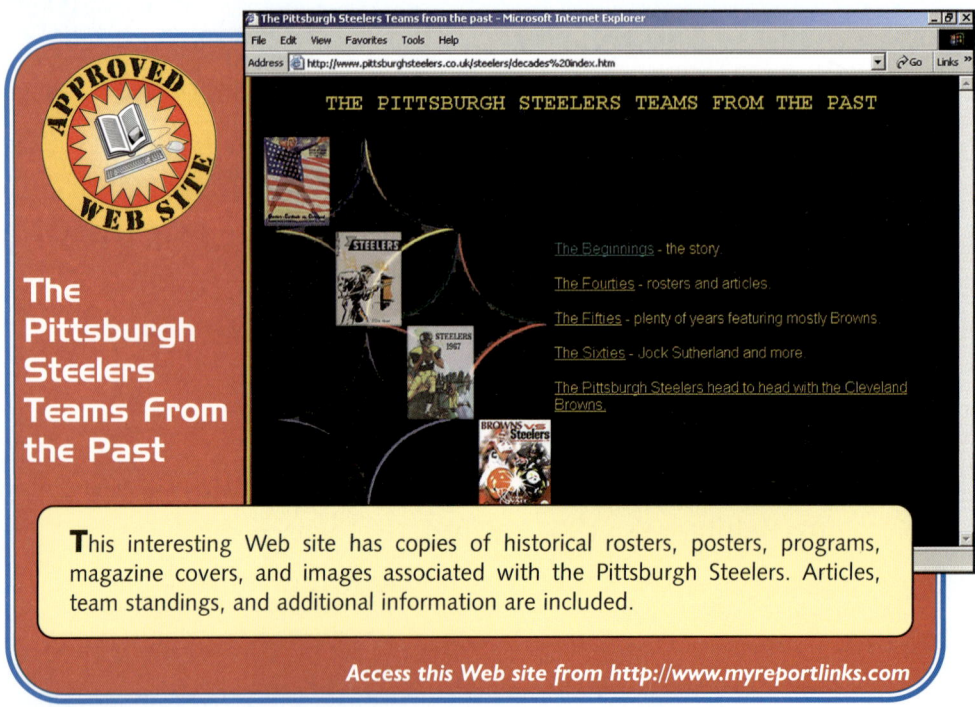

The Pittsburgh Steelers Teams From the Past

This interesting Web site has copies of historical rosters, posters, programs, magazine covers, and images associated with the Pittsburgh Steelers. Articles, team standings, and additional information are included.

Access this Web site from http://www.myreportlinks.com

At his first press conference, a reporter asked Noll if "respectability" was his goal for 1969. "Respectability?" he shot back. "Who wants to be respectable? That's spoken like a true loser. We're aiming for a championship now."[4]

Noll got off to a good start in the 1969 draft. In the first round, the Steelers selected defensive lineman Joe Greene. Though he had played in obscurity at North Texas State, "Mean Joe" was quick, powerful, and 275 pounds. Down in the tenth round, Pittsburgh snatched defensive end L. C. Greenwood out of tiny Arkansas-Pine Bluff. Together, Greene and Greenwood would anchor the Steelers line for more than a decade.

Four Decades of Futility

At his first team meeting in 1969, Chuck Noll mesmerized his players with his football insights. He outlined why the Steelers had lost so much: poor technique, too many mistakes. And he defined the formula for success: learn and execute the fundamentals, work for team goals.

Noll's Steelers won their first game in 1969, but they lost all the rest. Nevertheless, it was a tremendous learning experience for all involved. Noll learned which players were committed to team success. Those who were not would not be welcomed back. The players learned proper technique from Noll and his staff. Moreover, Greene's ferocious, fiery play set a good example for his teammates.

The Steelers may have gone 1–13, but they believed in Coach Noll and they believed in themselves. Their faith would be rewarded during the 1970s, the Steelers' decade of glory.

Quarterback Terry Bradshaw (No. 12) gives the touchdown signal as he celebrates with running backs Franco Harris (No. 32) and Sidney Thornton (No. 38). This score happened in the fourth quarter of Super Bowl XIV.

Stainless Steel Trophies

Long before the Chuck Noll era, Steelers coach Buddy Parker said: "When this team gets lucky, it'll be lucky for ten years."[1] His words would prove prophetic. During the 1970s, the Steelers would rule the NFL.

Pittsburgh's ten years of "luck" began on January 9, 1970. According to NFL rules, the team with the worst record in the league picks first in the following year's draft. Because Pittsburgh and Chicago had tied for the worst record in 1969, a coin toss was held on January 9 to determine who would select first. Dan Rooney and Noll attended for the Steelers, while Ed McCaskey represented the Bears. NFL Commissioner Pete Rozelle flipped a 1921 silver dollar. McCaskey called heads. The coin dropped to the floor, landing on tails. Pittsburgh would pick No. 1.

Afterward, Rooney gave the lucky coin to Noll. "I told him, 'This is the start of something big for us,'" Rooney said.[2]

Building Respect, Talent, and Pride

With the first pick in the draft, the Steelers selected quarterback Terry Bradshaw out of Louisiana Tech. Years earlier, Bradshaw had thrown a javelin 244 feet, 11 inches to set a national high school record. He could chuck a football nearly as far.

The Steelers improved considerably in 1970, their first season in Three Rivers Stadium. In addition to Greene, linebacker Andy Russell and cornerback Mel Blount shone on defense. In the season finale, running back John "Frenchy" Fuqua rushed for a team-record 218 yards. However, the team's 5–9 record pleased no one. Critics derided Bradshaw as a goofy "country bumpkin" who was not smart enough to lead a team.

In 1971, however, Noll found more building blocks in the NFL Draft. In the second round, he landed his kind of guy: Jack Ham. The young linebacker possessed tremendous instincts and savvy. When he was in the game, it was like having a coach on the field. In training camp, Noll continued with his businesslike approach to teaching football. By this point, he had earned the love and respect of virtually every one of his players.

Through ten games in 1971, the Steelers were 5–5 and tied for the Central Division lead. They finished 6–8, but NFL fans regarded them as a young, talented, up-and-coming team. All they needed, the Steelers thought, was a game-breaking running back—and a little more luck. Franco Harris would provide both in 1972.

Harris won over his teammates in training camp with his quick cuts and explosive bursts downfield. After several uneventful games, Harris emerged as a potent weapon. For six weeks in a row, he rushed for more than 100 yards, leading to five Pittsburgh victories.

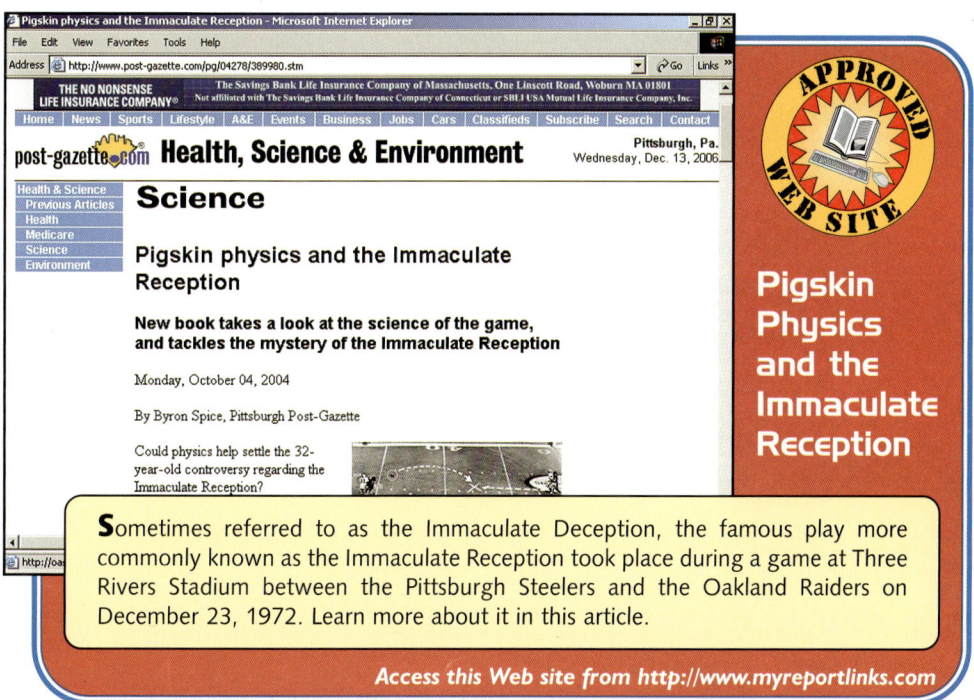

Pigskin Physics and the Immaculate Reception

Sometimes referred to as the Immaculate Deception, the famous play more commonly known as the Immaculate Reception took place during a game at Three Rivers Stadium between the Pittsburgh Steelers and the Oakland Raiders on December 23, 1972. Learn more about it in this article.

Access this Web site from http://www.myreportlinks.com

Harris meant the world to the Steelers. With teams keying on him, it took the pressure off Bradshaw. Pittsburgh's long drives also gave the defense time to rest. The Steelers amassed 343 points during the season, setting a team record. Fans packed Three Rivers Stadium. Groups called themselves "Franco's Italian Army," "Fuqua's Foreign Legion," and "Gerela's Gorillas" (after kicker Roy Gerela). On December 17, the Steelers won the first division title in the team's forty-year history. They finished 11–3.

The Immaculate Reception

Pittsburgh's first playoff game in twenty-five years turned into a classic. Hosting the Oakland Raiders, the Steelers trailed 7–6 with 22 seconds left. Facing fourth-and-ten from its own 40-yard line, Pittsburgh appeared doomed. Bradshaw dropped back to pass and fired over the middle. Running back John "Frenchy" Fuqua and Oakland safety Jack Tatum both converged on the ball, which ricocheted into the air.

The ball looked like it would fall incomplete, but out of nowhere came Franco Harris. The rookie snatched the pigskin just before it hit the ground and kept on running toward the end zone. The Raiders argued that the ball touched Fuqua before it fell into his teammate's hands—which would have made it an illegal reception. Even

Stainless Steel Trophies

Tatum, out of pathetic desperation, pleaded with Fuqua: "Tell them you touched it, Frenchy! Tell them you touched it!"[3]

But the officials could not determine if it had been Fuqua or Tatum who had touched the ball. The touchdown stood, and Pittsburgh prevailed 13–7. The Steelers would lose the following week, but fans would forever treasure the "Immaculate Reception."

Injuries plagued Bradshaw and Harris in 1973, but the Steelers still outscored their opponents 347–210. After winning the Central Division with

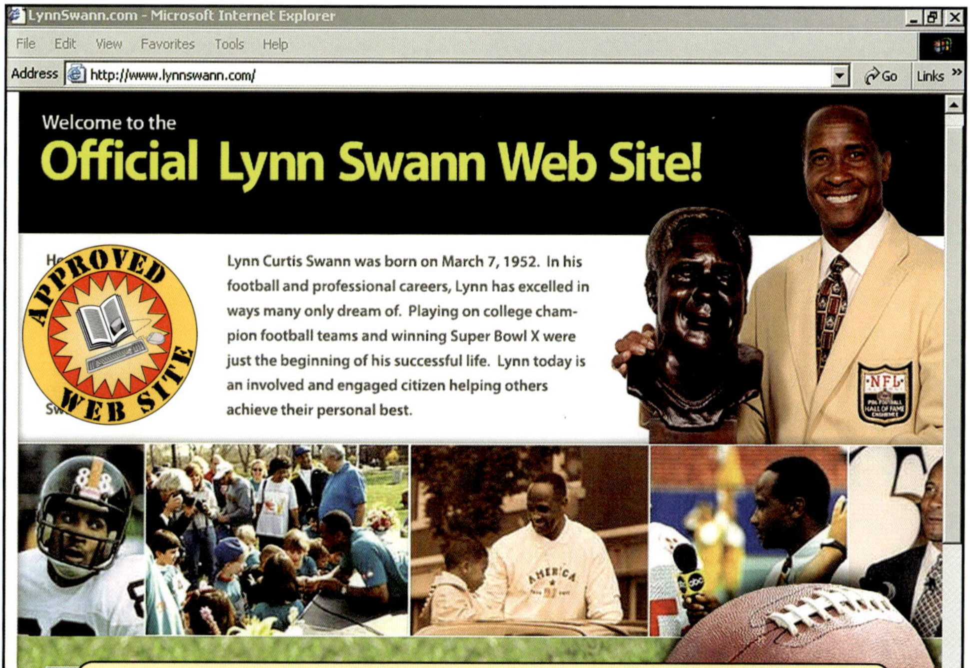

Lynn Swann played with the Pittsburgh Steelers as a wide receiver from 1974 to 1982. Swann went on to work with ABC Sports as a broadcaster. Read more about his life and career at **Welcome to the Official Lynn Swann Web Site!**

a 10–4 record, they lost to Oakland 33–14 in the first round of the playoffs. However, the Steelers would score their biggest victory of all during the 1974 NFL Draft.

On January 29, the first day of the two-day draft, the Steelers selected five players: wide receiver Lynn Swann, linebacker Jack Lambert, receiver John Stallworth, cornerback Jimmy Allen, and center Mike Webster. It was arguably the greatest draft day for any team in NFL history. With the exception of Allen, all of these players would be inducted into the Pro Football Hall of Fame.

Super Bowl Bound

These rookies would soon make an impact. Swann's acrobatic catches and Stallworth's sharp routes bolstered the passing attack. The tenacious Lambert helped fortify the "Steel Curtain" defense. In 1974, defensive linemen Joe Greene and L. C. Greenwood as well as linebackers Jack Ham and Andy Russell all went to the Pro Bowl. For the second time in three years, Greene was named NFL Defensive Player of the Year. Five times that season, Pittsburgh held opponents to seven or fewer points. With a 10–3–1 record, the Steelers stormed into the playoffs.

Pittsburgh opened against the Buffalo Bills and superstar halfback O. J. Simpson. The Steelers defense put the squeeze on "The Juice," limiting

Stainless Steel Trophies

▲ Lynn Swann hauls in a touchdown pass during a playoff game on January 4, 1975.

him to just 49 yards. Bradshaw and Swann starred as Pittsburgh rolled 32–14.

For the third straight season, the Steelers faced Oakland in the playoffs—this time for the AFC Championship. Playing in front of Oakland's notoriously hostile fans, Pittsburgh was a six-point underdog. Yet the Steel Curtain slammed hard on the Raiders offense, and Pittsburgh backs Franco Harris and Rocky Bleier rushed for a combined 209 yards. The Steelers won 24–13, to advance to the team's first Super Bowl in franchise history.

➲ Glory

In Super Bowl IX in New Orleans, the Steelers faced Minnesota's famous defense, known as the "Purple People Eaters." But it was the Pittsburgh defenders who ate purple-jerseyed people, specifically the Vikings' backfield. In the first quarter, Minnesota could muster only one first down. In the second, the Steelers tackled quarterback Fran Tarkenton in the end zone for a safety. The score was actually 2–0 at halftime.

In the second half, Pittsburgh scored on a 9-yard touchdown run by Harris and a short TD pass from Bradshaw to tight end Larry Brown. The Vikings' only score was a blocked punt returned for a touchdown, but they missed the extra point. In their 16–6 win, the Steelers defense set Super Bowl records for fewest first downs (9) and yards (119) allowed. Harris, meanwhile, ran for 158 yards to earn the MVP Award.

Yet that honor could have gone to the Steelers equipment manager. Tony Parisi had ordered special shoes for the players in case it rained, which it did. "I don't know where he got 'em, but it was like they came from heaven," said linebacker Andy Russell. "They made a tremendous difference."[4]

Afterward, the Steelers locker room was surprisingly quiet. But undeniably, emotions ran strong. Bleier, who had earned a Purple Heart during the Vietnam War, approached Rooney, who

Stainless Steel Trophies

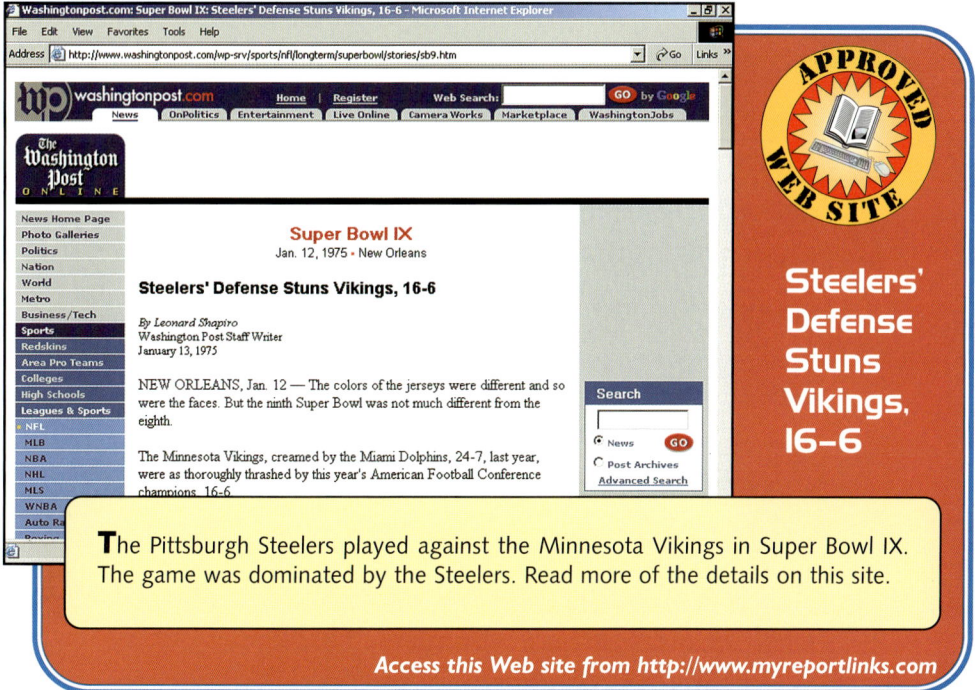

The Pittsburgh Steelers played against the Minnesota Vikings in Super Bowl IX. The game was dominated by the Steelers. Read more of the details on this site.

Access this Web site from http://www.myreportlinks.com

had stuck by his players for forty-two years. Bleier hugged the old man and whispered, "Thanks for giving me the chance to play." Rooney, like Rocky, choked back tears. "Thanks for being part of the championship team," Rooney said.[5]

When training camp arrived in 1975, Coach Noll was all business. He was determined not to let his team go soft after winning its first championship. "You had to go out there and win your job," said All-Pro L. C. Greenwood. "We didn't come into training camp and have Chuck say, 'OK, L. C., you're my starting defensive end.'"[6]

With his stellar young receivers, Bradshaw had his best year to date, completing 58 percent of his passes. Lynn Swann led the AFC with 11 TD receptions, and Franco Harris ran for 1,246 yards. Cornerback Mel Blount picked off 11 passes to lead the NFL. Incredibly, the Steelers sent eight defensive starters to the Pro Bowl. Pittsburgh finished 12–2, although their opening-round playoff opponent made fans uneasy.

Looney Tunes and America's Team

The Steelers hosted a Baltimore Colts team that had won its last nine games. Led by their "Looney Tunes" defensive line, the Colts had amassed a league-leading 59 sacks. The Steelers countered with an inspirational gimmick. Fans arrived waving "Terrible Towels," and the Steelers rose to the occasion. Pittsburgh romped, 28–10. To cap the scoring, thirty-five-year-old linebacker Andy Russell recovered a fumble and rambled 93 yards for a touchdown.

Pittsburgh hosted the rival Raiders in the AFC Championship Game. The field was frozen, and the windchill dipped to −12°F. This time Tony Parisi's wife came to the rescue, sewing hand-warming flaps to the Steelers' jerseys. Pittsburgh led 3–0 after three quarters and survived an eventful fourth period to win 16–10.

The Super Bowl in Miami was a marquee matchup. The reigning champion Steelers faced "America's Team," the Dallas Cowboys, who were playing in their third Super Bowl of the decade.

Stainless Steel Trophies

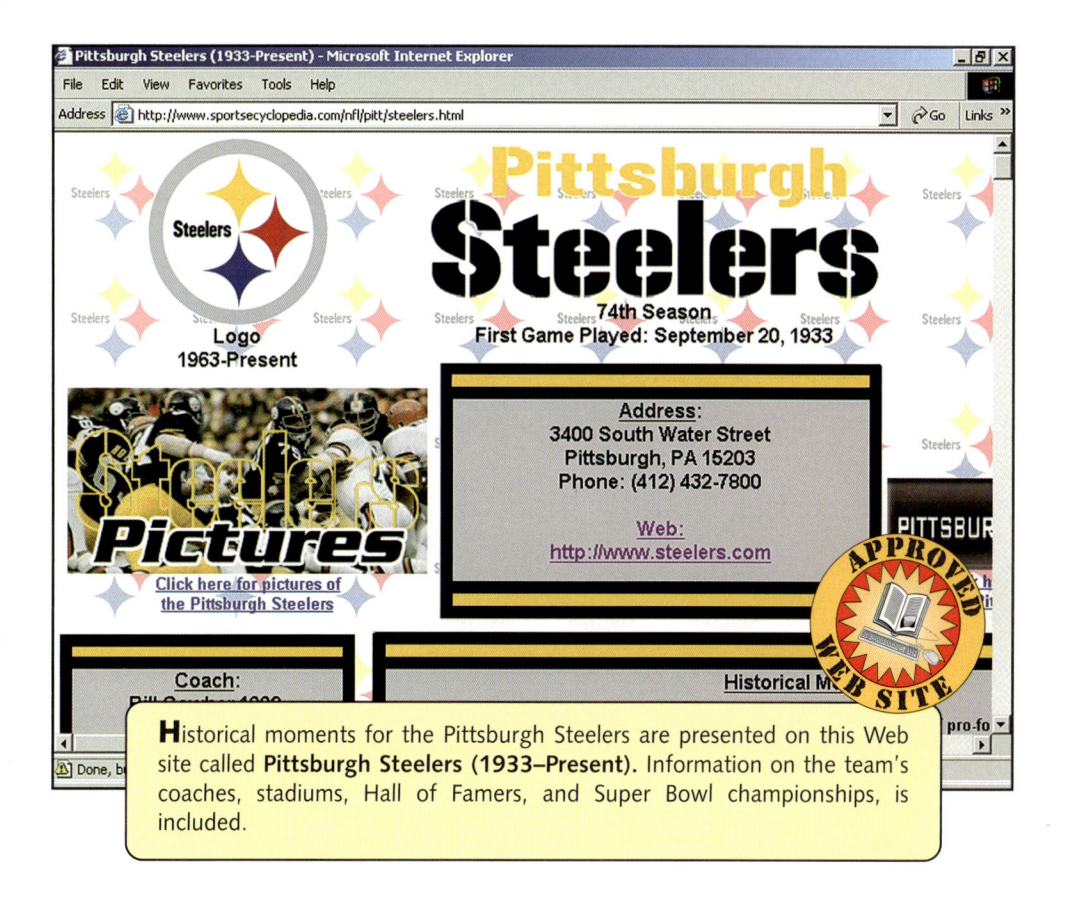

> Historical moments for the Pittsburgh Steelers are presented on this Web site called **Pittsburgh Steelers (1933–Present)**. Information on the team's coaches, stadiums, Hall of Famers, and Super Bowl championships, is included.

Quarterbacks Roger Staubach and Terry Bradshaw started hot, throwing touchdown passes in the first quarter. Dallas led 10–7 through three quarters, but the Steelers took over in the fourth. After blocking a punt in the end zone for a safety, Roy Gerela kicked two field goals to give Pittsburgh a 15–10 lead. With just over three minutes remaining, Bradshaw launched a 64-yard touchdown bomb to Swann. Despite a missed extra point, Pittsburgh held a seemingly comfortable 21–10 lead.

But Staubach, Dallas's "Captain Comeback," orchestrated a quick touchdown drive to make it

21–17. With 1:22 remaining, the Cowboys got the ball back. They moved to Pittsburgh's 38-yard line, but only seconds remained. Staubach had no choice but to heave two passes into the end zone. Jack Lambert broke up the first toss, Glen Edwards picked off the second, and the Steelers prevailed in one of the most exciting Super Bowls of all time.

Crushed Steel

Amazingly, the Steel Curtain was even more impenetrable in 1976. Again, eight defensive starters made the Pro Bowl. En route to a 10–4 record, Pittsburgh gave up the fewest points in the NFL—just 9.9 per game. Over the last nine contests, all wins, the Steelers allowed a total of 28 points. They recorded five shutouts during that stretch, including consecutive wins of 27–0, 23–0, and 45–0.

In the first round of the playoffs, Pittsburgh steamrolled the Baltimore Colts 40–14. However, injuries to Franco Harris and Rocky Bleier—each of whom had surpassed one thousand yards rushing on the year—prevented them from playing in the AFC Championship Game. The Raiders, of course, took no pity on their archrivals. Oakland cruised, 24–7, en route to its first Super Bowl title.

In 1977, the Steelers returned the familiar cast of characters: Bradshaw, Swann, Harris, and

Bleier on offense; Greene, Greenwood, Ham, and Lambert on defense. Though they won their sixth straight division title with a 9–5 record, a half-dozen other AFC teams were just as good. In the opening playoff game, the "Orange Crush" Denver Broncos flattened the Steelers 34–21.

Bradshaw Spells MVP

Those who predicted the Steelers' demise in 1978 underestimated the heart of this team. Coach Noll infused new talent into the defense, including linemen Steve Furness and John Banaszak, as well as defensive back Tony Dungy. But the man of the year in Pittsburgh was Terry Bradshaw. He paced the league with 28 touchdown passes and earned the NFL MVP Award. The Steelers started 7–0 and finished 14–2.

Bradshaw aired it out in the postseason, "crushing" Denver 33–10, and routing Houston 34–5. In the Super Bowl, the NFL's two superpowers clashed again. Both Pittsburgh and Dallas were looking to win their third Super Bowl of the decade. "We didn't like the Cowboys," Bradshaw said. "It was all the hype about them being 'America's Team.' We resented it."[7]

Cowboys linebacker Thomas "Hollywood" Henderson amplified the resentment. Henderson said that Bradshaw "couldn't spell cat if you spotted him the c and the a."[8]

Defensive tackle Mean Joe Greene runs over a blocker and puts himself in position to tackle Walt Garrison of the Dallas Cowboys.

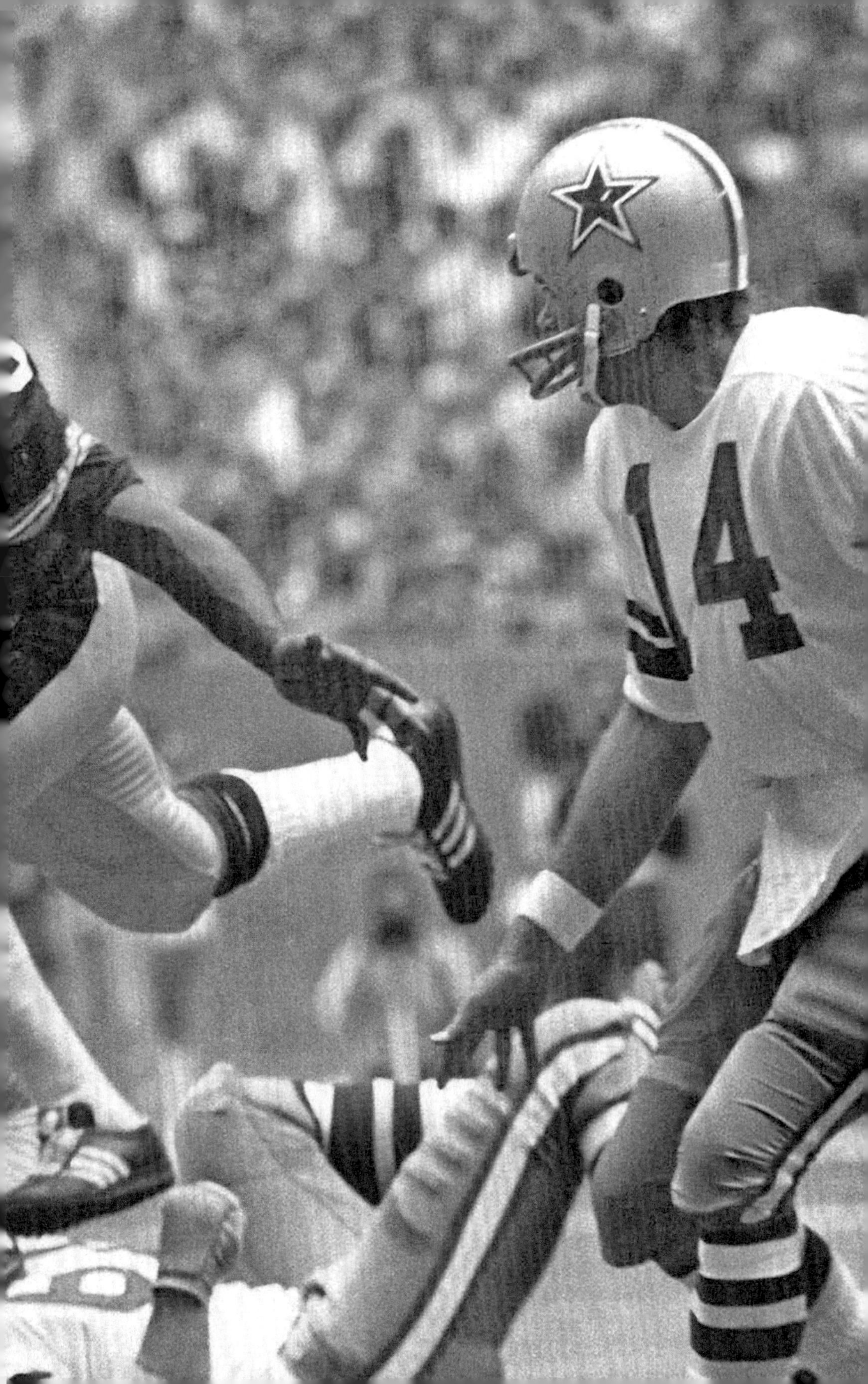
14

MyReportLinks.com Books

Henderson would later admit that he was high on drugs when he made that statement. Still, the quote was all over the media. Americans from coast to coast snickered about Bradshaw's alleged lack of intelligence. "But Terry handled it the right way," said Rocky Bleier. "He let his performance speak for him."[9]

Indeed, Bradshaw riddled the Dallas secondary during Super Bowl XIII. In the first half alone, he fired 3 touchdown passes to give Pittsburgh a 21–14 halftime lead. Chuck Noll's lucky silver dollar came into play in the third quarter. Dallas

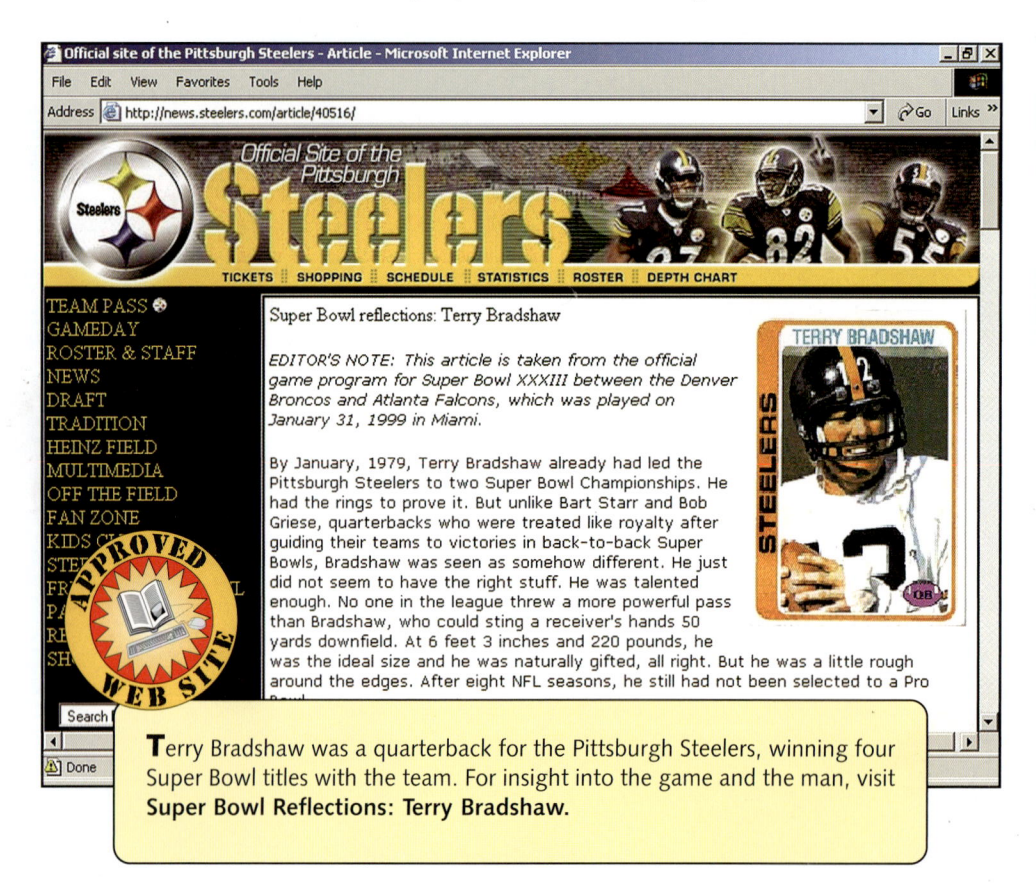

Terry Bradshaw was a quarterback for the Pittsburgh Steelers, winning four Super Bowl titles with the team. For insight into the game and the man, visit **Super Bowl Reflections: Terry Bradshaw.**

could have tied the score, but a wide-open Jackie Smith dropped a certain touchdown pass in the end zone. A Cowboys field goal made it 21–17.

In the fourth quarter, Bradshaw made a brilliant decision on third-and-nine. Anticipating a blitz, he changed the play at the last moment to a quick trap. Franco Harris blasted up the middle for a 22-yard touchdown. After a TD pass to Lynn Swann, Pittsburgh went up 35–17. Dallas scored twice late in the game, but the Steelers prevailed 35–31. They thus became the first team ever to win three Super Bowls.

By throwing for 4 touchdowns and a then Super Bowl-record 318 yards, Bradshaw was named the game's MVP. No more would anyone question his abilities. "I don't think any other quarterback could have done what Bradshaw did to us," said Dallas defensive end Harvey Martin. "We knocked him down, almost had him out at one point, but he came back. He deserved the MVP and everything he got after that game."[10]

Gunning for No. 4

By 1979, fans again questioned whether the Steelers had grown too old. Ten of their starters were over thirty. However, Chuck Noll's men executed well enough to compensate for the loss of athleticism. In fact, they led the league in both yards gained (6,258) and fewest allowed (4,621).

Pittsburgh finished 12–4 and won its eighth straight Central Division title.

In the playoffs, the Steelers easily disposed of Miami, 34–14. In the next game, experts considered Houston one of the two best teams in the NFL, but Pittsburgh breezed to a 27–13 win. Everyone shared the same thought for Super Bowl XIV: Heaven help the Los Angeles Rams. During

▲ Jack Ham (No. 59) of the Pittsburgh Steelers wraps up Doug Dennison of the Cowboys in this action photo from Super Bowl X. J. T. Thomas of the Steelers is entering the picture from the left.

Stainless Steel Trophies

You will find an incredible amount of information on past Super Bowl and playoff histories, including highlights, recaps, MVPs, records, and standings, on the **SuperBowl.com** Web site.

EDITOR'S CHOICE

the season, Los Angeles had gone 9–7 and outscored its opponents by just fourteen points. Though the Super Bowl would be staged in the Rams' backyard—the Rose Bowl in Pasadena—the Steelers were favored by 10 1/2 points.

Nevertheless, the game turned into a nail-biter. Six times the lead changed hands. Los Angeles led 13–10 at the half, but Swann turned an acrobatic catch into a 47-yard touchdown. By the end of the third period, however, the Rams moved ahead 19–17. Early in the fourth quarter, Bradshaw struck like lightning. His downfield pass to John Stallworth resulted in a 73-yard touchdown. Franco Harris's one-yard touchdown run sealed the Steelers' 31–19 victory. Bradshaw, with 309 yards passing, earned his second straight Super Bowl MVP Award.

Buddy Parker's "ten years of luck" prediction had come true, as the 1970s Steelers won four Super Bowl titles. Eerily, the fourth crown came ten years to the month after the "lucky coin" flip, which had given Pittsburgh the opportunity to draft Bradshaw.

In reality, of course, the Steelers' success had little to do with luck. The dynasty was built on discipline, hard work, and smart decisions. "It all boils down to one person," said Joe Greene. "Charles Henry Noll. This is his team. He built it. He taught us how to win, how to keep winning. There aren't any indispensable Steelers, just Chuck."[11]

A Bare Thumb

By the 1980 season, Steelers fans had become greedy. The motto around Pittsburgh was "One for the Thumb," meaning a fifth Super Bowl ring. But the great Steelers dynasty had run out of steam. From 1980 to 1982, Bradshaw, Harris, and what remained of the Steel Curtain defense led the Pittsburgh Steelers to records of 9–7, 8–8, and a strike-shortened 6–3. But the Steelers made the playoffs only in 1982, when they lost a heartbreaking elimination game to San Diego.

By the end of the 1982 season, Mean Joe Greene, Jack Ham, and Lynn Swann had all retired. With Bradshaw injured in 1983, Cliff Stoudt took over as quarterback. Despite his 21 interceptions (and just 12 touchdown passes), the Steelers made the playoffs at 10–6. But they lost to the Los Angeles Raiders 38–10, and then lost Bradshaw and star cornerback Mel Blount to retirement. Franco Harris moved on to Seattle.

For the rest of the 1980s, the Steelers wallowed in mediocrity. Their blunder in the 1983 draft,

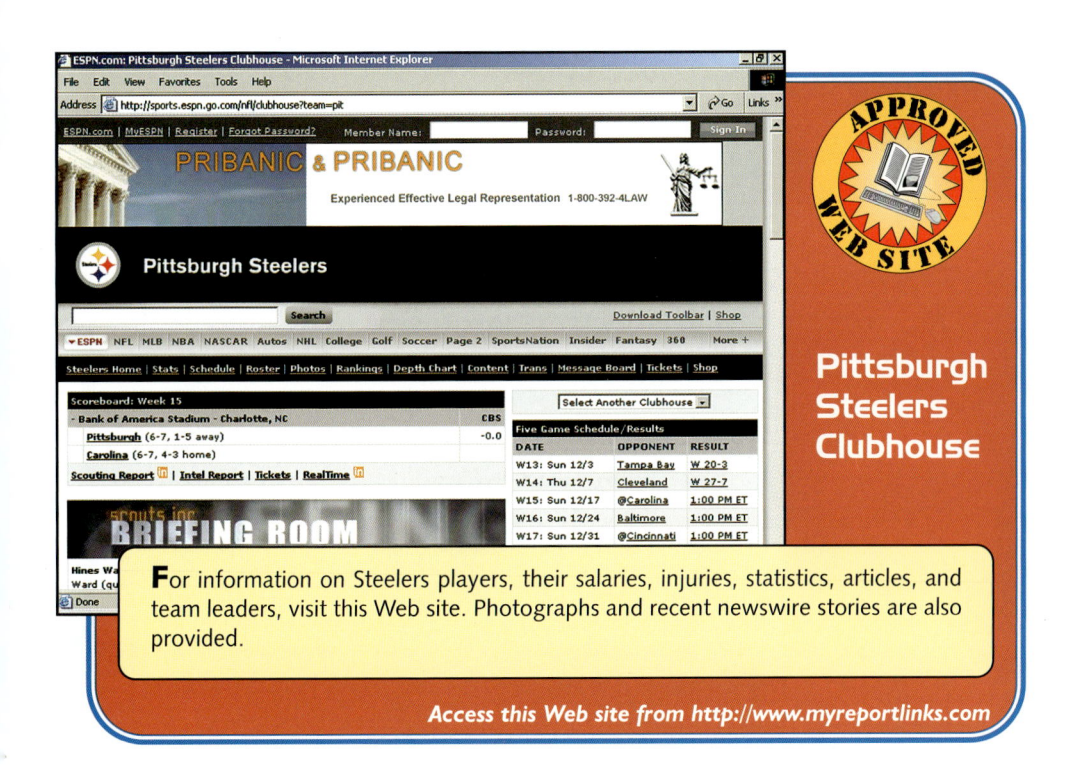

Pittsburgh Steelers Clubhouse

For information on Steelers players, their salaries, injuries, statistics, articles, and team leaders, visit this Web site. Photographs and recent newswire stories are also provided.

Access this Web site from http://www.myreportlinks.com

when they passed on quarterback Dan Marino, proved costly. Marino would become the most prolific passer of all time, while Pittsburgh QB Mark Malone proved no better than ordinary from 1984 to 1987. The Steelers made the playoffs at 9–7 in 1984, and even beat Denver in that year's postseason. But after a 45–28 loss to Marino and Miami in the 1984 AFC Championship Game, the decline began. Beginning in 1985, Pittsburgh went 7–9, 6–10, 8–7, and 5–11.

In 1989, the Steelers were one of the worst teams ever to make the playoffs. Though 9–7, they

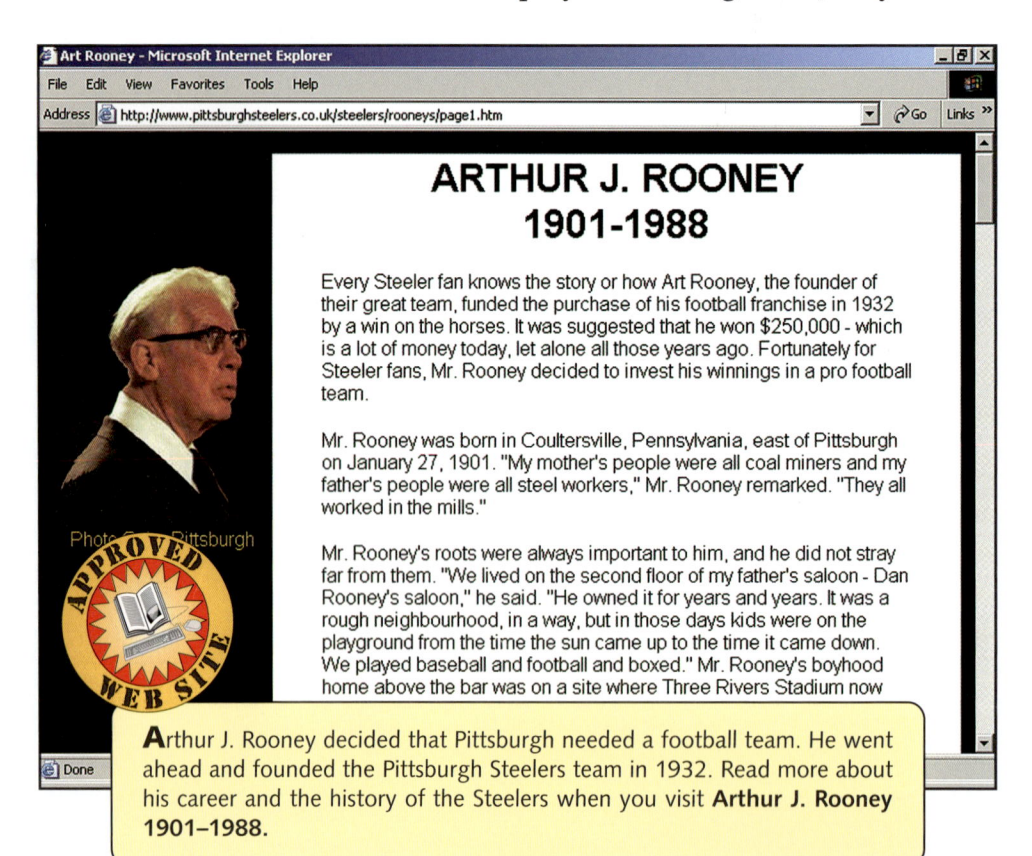

Arthur J. Rooney decided that Pittsburgh needed a football team. He went ahead and founded the Pittsburgh Steelers team in 1932. Read more about his career and the history of the Steelers when you visit **Arthur J. Rooney 1901–1988.**

were outscored 326–265. Starting quarterback Bubby Brister threw only 9 touchdown passes. Leading rusher Tim Worley averaged just 3.9 yards per carry. They lost on opening day to Cleveland, 51–0—at home! And yet in their first playoff game, they roared from behind to tie Houston, then won 26–23 in overtime. They could have beaten Denver the next week, but quarterback John Elway pulled out a 24–23 victory in the closing moments.

In 1990, Pittsburgh improved significantly, leading the NFL in fewest yards allowed. Spearheaded by cornerback Rod Woodson, the Steelers yielded just 9 touchdown passes while intercepting 24. Along with Houston and Cincinnati, Pittsburgh tied for first place in the Central Division at 9–7. But due to the tiebreaking formula, the Oilers and Bengals made the playoffs and the Steelers watched the postseason on television.

Chuck Noll remained Pittsburgh's coach, but his silver dollar had run out of luck. After a 7–9 campaign in 1991, he retired. The Steelers thus faced a new challenge: replacing the only four-time champion Super Bowl coach in NFL history.

Bill Cowher gives some words of praise to one of his players after a touchdown score. Cowher continued Pittsburgh's winning tradition after taking over from Chuck Noll.

The Power of Cowher

Less than one day after being named Steelers head coach, Bill Cowher thought about backing out. It was January 21, 1992, and the pressure and media attention seemed overwhelming. "This is unbelievable," he told his wife. "If every day is like this day, I don't know if I can do this. Honey, I may have gotten myself in too deep over my head."[1]

Perhaps the Steelers had chosen too young a man. Cowher, the former defensive coordinator with the Kansas City Chiefs, was just thirty-four years old. Yet he was too good to pass up. He brought an emotional intensity to his job that players found inspiring.

Wanting to establish the running game in 1992, Cowher put his faith in little-known back Barry Foster. Foster, strong and quick, responded with 1,690 yards rushing, second most in the NFL.

Though the Steelers were expected to finish last in their division, they instead won the AFC Central with a record of 11–5. Cowher, the youngest field boss in the league, was named NFL Coach of the Year. Only a 24–3 loss to Buffalo in their first playoff game tarnished the season.

Could it be Number Five?

By 1993, Steel City fans believed a Super Bowl could be in the cards. That fall, quarterback Neil O'Donnell fired 14 touchdown passes and just 7 interceptions. Kicker Gary Anderson boomed 28 field goals and missed just two. Pittsburgh made the playoffs at 9–7, but heartache followed in the opening playoff game. With Pittsburgh leading Kansas City 24–17, Chiefs quarterback Joe Montana completed a fourth-down touchdown pass late in the game. The Chiefs ended the Steelers' season with a field goal in overtime.

In 1994, the Steelers seemed to put it all together. Foster and John L. Williams each topped eight hundred yards rushing. Led by cornerback Rod Woodson and sack master Kevin Greene, the defense allowed just 19 touchdowns—fewest in the NFL. Pittsburgh finished 12–4 and blew out Cleveland 29–9 in the playoffs.

In the AFC Championship Game, Pittsburgh was favored by 8 1/2 points over San Diego. Before the game, the Steelers were even making plans to produce a Super Bowl video. Pittsburgh held a 13–3 lead in the third quarter, but the Chargers struck back with 2 touchdown passes. The Steelers had a chance to win late in the game, but a fourth-down pass from the 3-yard line was batted down. Chided San Diego safety Stanley Richard, "I wonder what these guys are going to do with their Super Bowl video now?"[2] The answer? Save it for next year.

Super Bowl Revisited

Pittsburgh bounced back strong in 1995. O'Donnell found a new favorite receiver, Yancey Thigpen, who amassed 1,307 yards in receiving yardage. The Steelers won eight in a row and finished 11–5. After routing Buffalo 40–21, Pittsburgh entered the AFC Championship Game as an eleven-point favorite. Like the previous year, the game came down to one play. Trailing 20–16 at Pittsburgh's 29-yard line, the Colts' Jim Harbaugh lofted a pass toward the end zone. After several deflections, Steelers defensive back Randy Fuller batted it away, sending Pittsburgh to Tempe, Arizona, for Super Bowl XXX.

Unfortunately for the Steelers, the odds were stacked against them. The NFC had won the last eleven Super Bowls, and the star-studded Dallas Cowboys were favored by 13 1/2 points. Trailing 20–17 in the fourth quarter, Pittsburgh had the

MyReportLinks.com Books

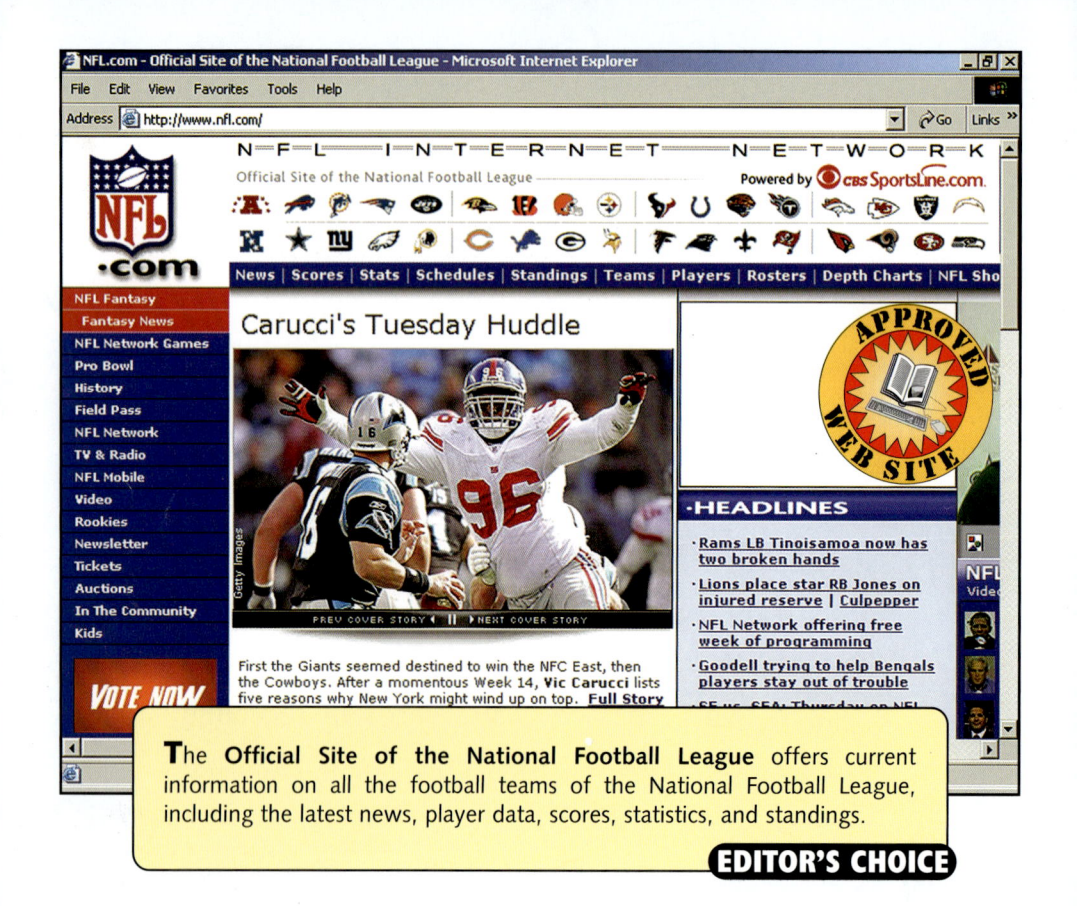

The Official Site of the National Football League offers current information on all the football teams of the National Football League, including the latest news, player data, scores, statistics, and standings.

EDITOR'S CHOICE

ball with four minutes left, but one bad pass proved deadly. Dallas's Larry Brown picked off an O'Donnell pass and returned it 33 yards to the Steelers' 6-yard line. An Emmitt Smith touchdown run clinched a 27–17 Cowboys victory.

While some fans blamed O'Donnell for the loss, Cowher stood by his side. "Neil got us here," Cowher said. "Without Neil O'Donnell, we wouldn't be playing at the last of January. Look at the big picture. Don't look at the small picture."[3]

O'Donnell, however, would never play another game for Pittsburgh. After the season, he left as a free agent. QB Mike Tomczak proved an adequate replacement, but the big story in 1996 was the acquisition of Jerome Bettis from the St. Louis Rams. A massive running back, "The Bus" plowed over opponents for 1,431 yards in 1996. The Steelers finished 10–6 and crushed the Colts 42–14 in the AFC Wildcard Game. New England, however, humbled Cowher's men the next week, winning 28–3.

In 1997, quarterback Kordell Stewart added a new dimension to the Steelers offense. A brilliant athlete, Stewart rushed for 476 yards and 11 touchdowns while also throwing for 21 scores. With The Bus enjoying his greatest season (1,665 yards rushing), Pittsburgh finished 11–5. In the divisional playoff game, the Steelers beat New England in a defensive war, 7–6. In the AFC Championship Game, Denver scored 2 touchdowns after the first half's two-minute warning. That was the difference as the Broncos prevailed 24–21.

The Unlucky Coin

While the 1970 coin toss had proved magical for the Steelers, a coin flipped in 1998 seemed to be cursed. Pittsburgh opened the season at 7–4, but their Thanksgiving game at Detroit went to overtime. A coin toss would determine who would

MyReportLinks.com Books

Neil O'Donnell is shown here warming up before taking the field for Super Bowl XXX.

receive the kickoff in sudden death. Bettis appeared to call tails, but referee Phil Luckett misheard him and said, "Heads is the call. He said heads. It is tails."[4] Bettis and the Steelers protested, but to no avail. Detroit received the kickoff and scored on its first possession. Cursed or not, Pittsburgh lost its last five games and missed the playoffs.

Bad breaks continued in 1999, mostly due to the Steelers' sloppy play. Stewart lost his starting job to Tomczak, and Pittsburgh finished 6–10. In 2000, fans said their farewells to Three Rivers Stadium. The team would leave the dull, circular concrete structure after the season. On the field, Bettis (1,341 yards) and the defense carried the team. During a four-game stretch, Pittsburgh won by the scores of 20–3, 15–0, 22–0, and 9–6. However, their 9–7 overall record was not good enough to make the playoffs.

The Power of Cowher

➡ Can Not Win the Big One

The Steelers' move into Heinz Field in 2001 seemed to revitalize Cowher's troops. Stewart completed 60 percent of his passes, while Bettis topped 1,000 yards for the sixth straight season. Young receivers Hines Ward and Plaxico Burress each eclipsed 1,000 yards in receiving yardage. Linebacker Kendrell Bell, the NFL Defensive Rookie of the Year, contributed to the stingiest defense in the NFL. With a 13–3 record, and an easy 27–10 win over the Baltimore Ravens, Pittsburgh hosted its fourth AFC Championship Game in eight years.

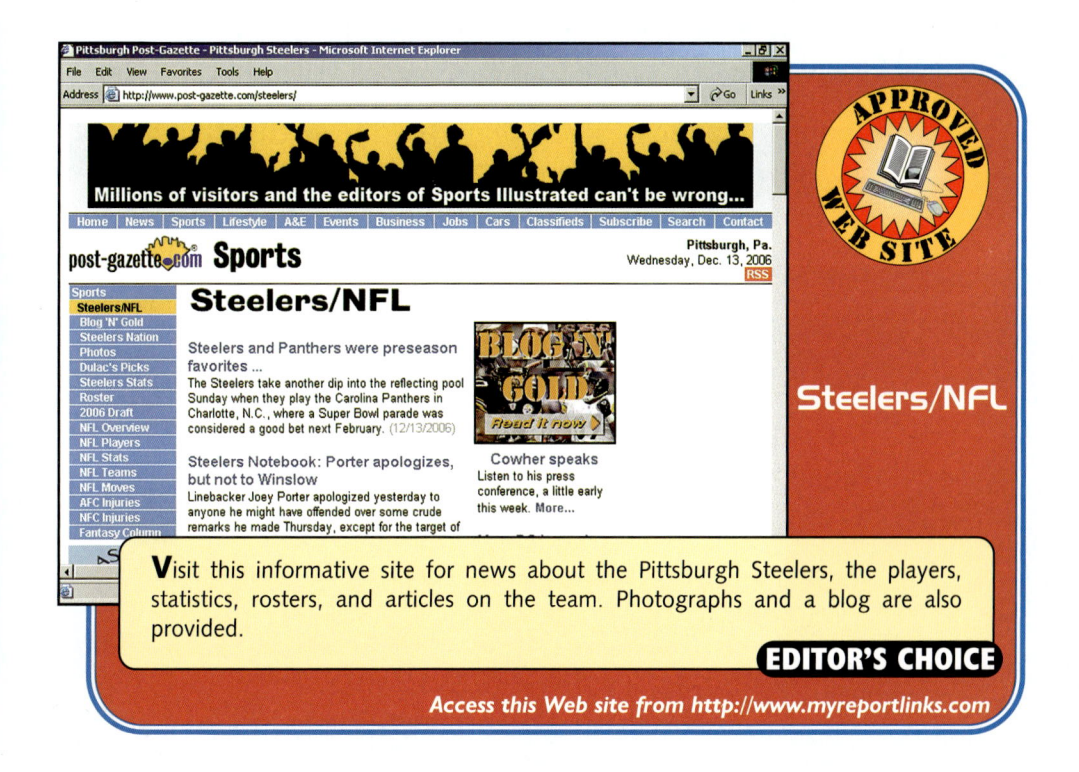

Visit this informative site for news about the Pittsburgh Steelers, the players, statistics, rosters, and articles on the team. Photographs and a blog are also provided.

EDITOR'S CHOICE

Access this Web site from http://www.myreportlinks.com

Against the New England Patriots, the Steelers were nine-point favorites. "I would have bet my whole season's salary we would win," said Pittsburgh safety Lee Flowers.[5] Thank goodness he was not a betting man. Poor execution doomed the Steelers. The Patriots returned a punt and a blocked field goal for touchdowns to take a 21–3 lead. Pittsburgh cut the deficit to 24–17, but Stewart threw 2 interceptions in the final three minutes. With three losses in four recent AFC Championship Games, all at home, the Steelers were now known as the team that could not win the big one.

Thrills and Chills

Though Stewart made the Pro Bowl in 2001, he lost his job to a journeyman the following fall. Tommy Maddox, a ten-year backup in the NFL, took the quarterback reins. Surprisingly, 2002 turned into an aerial circus—on both sides of the ball. Maddox and Stewart completed 64 percent of their passes for a combined 4,036 yards. Hines and Burress each surpassed 1,300 yards in receiving. Teams could not run on Pittsburgh, but they found success through the air.

The Steelers made the playoffs at 10–5–1, and their first postseason game was a high-scoring donnybrook. Cleveland held a 24–7 lead with just 19 minutes to go, but Maddox and the Steelers remained composed. "We have time, so don't

The Power of Cowher

The Story Behind the Pittsburgh Steelers Logo

The Pittsburgh Steelers logo has three four-pointed star-like shapes encased in a circle. Owner Art Rooney began using this Steelmark for his team in 1962. More details are available to you on the site.

EDITOR'S CHOICE

Access this Web site from http://www.myreportlinks.com

panic," said offensive coordinator Mike Mularkey.[6] Maddox responded with 3 touchdown drives over the next 16 minutes, cutting the deficit to 33–28. With fifty-four seconds remaining, Steelers power back Chris Fuamatu-Ma'afala electrified Heinz Field with a 3-yard touchdown run. Pittsburgh was moving on.

In the AFC Divisional Playoff Game, Maddox again rallied the troops. Pittsburgh overcame a 14–0 hole against Tennessee to tie the game 31–31 at the end of regulation. It then came down to one controversial penalty. Titans kicker Joe Nedney missed a 31-yard field goal attempt, but Pittsburgh's Dewayne Washington was flagged for running into the kicker. Nedney then split the uprights from 26 yards out. "For a game to be decided on that call is ludicrous," fumed coach Cowher. "A game can't be decided because a kicker takes two steps and we have someone slide into him."[7] But it was. For the twenty-third consecutive season, the Steelers failed to win "One for the Thumb."

Pittsburgh fell to 6–10 in 2003 mostly because they could not run the football. The team's 3.24 yards per carry ranked dead last in the NFL. Yet the Steelers also were looking for young blood at quarterback—someone who could serve as an apprentice to the aging Maddox. They found him in the 2004 NFL Draft. With the eleventh pick in the first round, Pittsburgh took a six-foot five-inch, 240-pound gunslinger from Miami University of Ohio named Ben Roethlisberger.

The Unbeatable Rookie

In the second game of the 2004 season, Maddox left with an elbow injury. The Steelers were on their way to defeat, but Roethlisberger looked good coming off the bench. "I'm not Tommy Maddox; can't be Tommy Maddox," Roethlisberger said. "I'm just going to do the best that I can."[8] He proceeded to lead Pittsburgh to 14 straight wins.

NFL fans sat back in amazement as the kid QB helped Pittsburgh become the first AFC team ever to go 15–1. "Big Ben" ended New England's

21-game win streak, prevailing 34–20. A week later, he beat the undefeated Philadelphia Eagles (7–0), 27–3. Of course, he had plenty of help. The Steelers sent two offensive linemen to the Pro Bowl, and the defense yielded the fewest yards in the NFL. Roethlisberger smashed numerous rookie records, including the highest passer rating (98.1) ever by an NFL rookie.

Only in the playoffs did Roethlisberger stumble, as he threw 2 interceptions against New York. The Jets would have pulled off the upset had Doug Brien not missed two field goals in the last two

Ben Roethlisberger is the quarterback for the Pittsburgh Steelers. His bio, latest news, and blog can be accessed when you visit his multimedia Web site called **Big Ben 7: Welcome to the Official Website of Super Bowl Champion Ben Roethlisberger.**

minutes. Jeff Reed's overtime field goal won it for the Steelers, 20–17, sending them to the AFC Championship Game. But with Roethlisberger's 3 interceptions against powerful New England, Pittsburgh did not have a chance. The Patriots won 41–27, ending Pittsburgh's winning streak at 15. It was also the Steelers' fourth loss in the AFC title game in eleven seasons—all on their home turf.

Bettis, who fumbled twice in the playoffs, contemplated retirement. But Roethlisberger helped convince him to come back for one more season. The result was pure magic.

"Once in a Blue Moon"

Pittsburgh opened the 2005 season at 7–2. The playoffs seemed assured until they lost three straight games. At 7–5 in the tough AFC, the Steelers needed a lift down the stretch. They got it from their nails-tough linebackers.

In 2005, Pittsburgh's Joey Porter led all NFL linebackers with 10.5 quarterback sacks. Steelers linebacker Clark Haggans was right behind with 9 sacks, while linebacker James Farrior led Pittsburgh with 119 tackles. Over the next three games, the Steelers held their opponents to 9, 3, and 0 points. In the final game, Pittsburgh whipped Detroit 35–21. Bettis rumbled for 3 touchdowns, and Willie Parker ran for 135 yards—giving him 1,202 for the season. The Steelers made

The Power of Cowher

the playoffs as the No. 6 seed in the AFC. They would have to win two games on the road just to make the conference championship game—a feat no AFC team had ever accomplished.

Pittsburgh got a break early in its first playoff game. Carson Palmer, Cincinnati's All-Pro quarterback, left with a serious knee injury. With Roethlisberger razor sharp (14-of-19, 3 touchdowns), the Bengals could not recover. The Steelers won 31–17. Their next game would go down as one of the wildest in NFL playoff history.

Through fifty-five minutes, Pittsburgh

Ben Roethlisberger reaches back to throw a pass during the AFC Championship game on January 22, 2006.

held a 21–10 lead over Indianapolis (which had started the season 13–0 and finished 14–2). Steelers safety Troy Polamalu seemed to clinch the game with an interception, but he fumbled it away on a controversial call. Indy came back to score on an Edgerrin James touchdown run. A two-point conversion pass made it 21–18.

With 1:20 remaining, Colts quarterback Peyton Manning was sacked on fourth down at his own 2-yard line. Colts fans headed for the exits . . . only to stop in their tracks when Bettis stunningly fumbled on the next play. Colts cornerback Nick Harper scooped up the loose ball and sprinted downfield. Roethlisberger saved a probable game-winning touchdown with a lunging tackle on Indy's 42-yard line. "Once in a blue moon, Jerome fumbles," said Roethlisberger. "Once in a blue moon, I make a tackle. They just happened to be in the same game."[9] On the same play. Colts kicker Mike Vanderjagt could have tied it with a last-chance field goal, but his 46-yard attempt sailed wide right. The Steelers escaped, 21–18.

One For the Thumb

Roethlisberger, whose interceptions had doomed the Steelers in the previous year's AFC Championship, redeemed himself on January 22, 2006. Though an underdog against the Denver Broncos, Pittsburgh breezed, 34–17. Roethlisberger

The Power of Cowher

The Pro Football Hall of Fame is actually the NFL's Hall of Fame. It is located in Canton, Ohio, and opened on September 7, 1963. Take an online tour and learn more about football and its best players when you visit the **Pro Football Hall of Fame** Web site.

EDITOR'S CHOICE

completed 21-of-29 for 275 yards, 2 touchdowns, and no interceptions. The Steelers had pulled off an unparalleled feat—three straight playoff road wins—and were headed to the Super Bowl.

Though Detroit hosted the Super Bowl, about 80 percent of the crowd rooted for the Steelers. These diehards were glad to travel the three hundred miles and pay hundreds (or thousands) of dollars for tickets. Of course, they brought with them their "Terrible Towels."

In Super Bowl XL, Pittsburgh faced the Seattle Seahawks, who had scored an NFL-high 452 points during the season. Shaun Alexander had rushed for 1,880 yards and an NFL-record 28 touchdowns. Nevertheless, Pittsburgh was favored by eleven points.

Late in the first half, Roethlisberger's goal-line plunge put Pittsburgh up 7–3. After the legendary Rolling Stones performed at halftime, the second half rocked. The Steelers' Willie Parker ripped off a 75-yard touchdown run (a Super Bowl record) to make it a 14–3 lead. Kelly Herndon of the

◀ Willie Parker carries the ball during a playoff game against the Indianapolis Colts on January 15, 2006. Parker then played a crucial role in the Steelers Super Bowl XL victory.

Seahawks returned an interception 76 yards to the Pittsburgh 20. Seattle punched it in to make it 14–10.

With nine minutes to go, the Steelers scored on a spectacular trick play. Roethlisberger pitched the ball to Parker, who handed off to Antwaan Randle El. As the Seattle defense keyed on the speedy receiver, he shocked the house by lofting a 43-yard touchdown pass to Hines Ward. At 20 million Super Bowl parties across America, fans went wild. The extra point made it 21–10, and that is how it ended.

Bettis, playing his last NFL game, attracted most of the attention. But head coach Bill Cowher did not forget seventy-three-year-old Steelers owner Dan Rooney. Cowher handed his boss the Vince Lombardi Trophy signifying the Super Bowl championship. "I've been waiting a long time to do this," Cowher said. "This is yours, man."[10]

Back in Pittsburgh, thousands of fans flooded the streets. They sang Steelers songs and waved their Terrible Towels. After twenty-six years, they finally had One for the Thumb.

Art Rooney, Steelers founder and president, looks through a program in the locker room prior to Super Bowl X.

The Masterminds 5

Many team owners talk about the importance of loyalty, but no one backs it up like the Pittsburgh Steelers. Here is a team owned by the Rooney family for seventy-three years. From 1970 to 2007, they changed head coaches only once. Moreover, the "Voice of the Steelers" manned the mic through seven presidential administrations. Profiled here are six men who helped lay the foundation for Steelers football.

Art Rooney

As the Steelers celebrated their first Super Bowl victory in 1975, the players gathered around the team's seventy-three-year-old owner. Linebacker Andy Russell handed him the game ball. "This one's for The Chief," Russell said. "It's been a long time coming."[1]

MyReportLinks.com Books

Art Rooney was a lifelong native of Pennsylvania. He descended from coal miners and steelworkers, and his father owned a saloon. Rooney ran a successful semipro football team, and in 1933 he purchased an NFL franchise—the Pittsburgh Pirates.

For years, the Pirates (who were later renamed the Steelers) lost too many games and too much money. But Rooney, who won $256,000 at the racetrack on a magical day in 1936, kept the franchise afloat. Through 1971, his team enjoyed only six winning seasons and never won a playoff

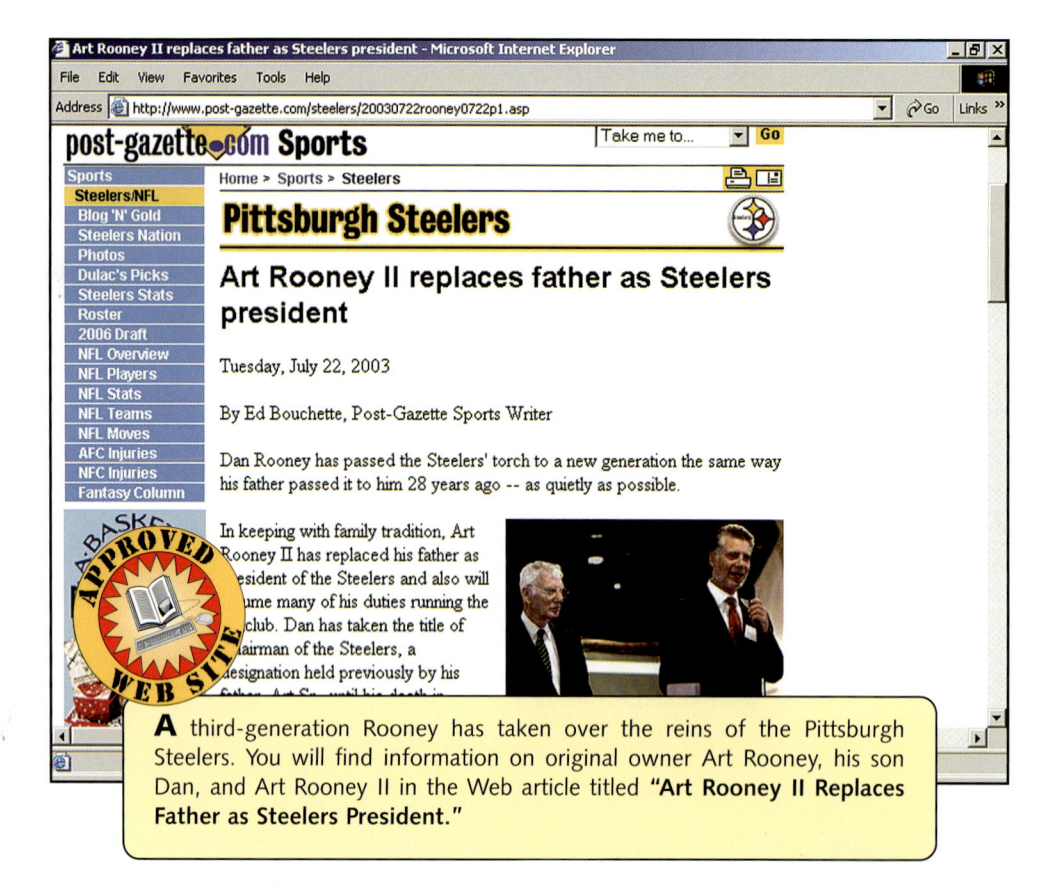

▲ A third-generation Rooney has taken over the reins of the Pittsburgh Steelers. You will find information on original owner Art Rooney, his son Dan, and Art Rooney II in the Web article titled **"Art Rooney II Replaces Father as Steelers President."**

game. Still, those throughout the organization and the city adored the kindly team owner.

"We all knew and loved The Chief," said Sophie Masloff, a former mayor of Pittsburgh. "He stopped to talk to everyone. To Art Rooney, everyone he met was someone special. He made you feel important."[2]

Rooney entered the 1970s as the NFL's biggest loser, but he closed the decade with more career Super Bowl rings than any other owner. To this day, his spirit lives throughout the Steelers community. Every football Sunday, fans file past a bronze statue of The Chief outside Heinz Field.

Dan Rooney

The son of team owner Art Rooney, Dan Rooney literally grew up with the Steelers. He served as water boy at age fourteen, and before long he was negotiating contracts with the players. "I was too young to sign the contracts—I was only 18 or 19 at the time—so I would have to take the contracts in to the coach to get them signed after I worked them out," he said.[3]

After earning his college degree in 1955, Rooney rejoined the Steelers front office. With a mind for both football and business, he quickly earned admiration around the NFL. He treated players with respect and warmth, contributing to a family-like atmosphere. Rooney was the visionary who signed head coach Chuck Noll, and later Bill Cowher.

Dan Rooney became Steelers president in 1975 and upon the death of his father in 1988, team owner. Twelve years later, he joined Art Rooney, Sr., in the Pro Football Hall of Fame.

Buddy Parker

Pittsburgh was abuzz in August 1957 when the Steelers hired Ray "Buddy" Parker as head coach.

▲ The Steelers held a welcome-home ceremony for Terry Bradshaw on October 21, 2002. Steelers owner Dan Rooney is shown here sharing a laugh with the former quarterback.

Parker had taken the Detroit Lions to the NFL Championship Game three times in the 1950s, winning twice. Could he do the same for the Steelers, who had not won a playoff game in their twenty-four-year existence?

Sadly, not even Parker could save this woeful franchise. He coached Pittsburgh for eight seasons, posting such impressive records as 7–4–1, 9–5, and 7–4–3. Yet, not once did the Steelers make the playoffs.

Parker gambled the future for the present, trading draft picks for veterans. In 1958, he traded up-and-coming quarterback Earl Morrall and two first-round picks to the Lions for legendary quarterback Bobby Layne. Layne served nobly for five seasons but could not recapture his championship magic.

After the team slumped to 5–9 in 1964, Parker signed a new contract with the Steelers. But after they lost their four preseason games in 1965, he abruptly quit. Reportedly, he was upset at Steelers owner Art Rooney for not letting him make a trade.[4] No one else could win with the team either. Over the rest of the decade, the Steelers went 14–53–3.

Chuck Noll

It was the first day of training camp in 1969, and head coach Chuck Noll addressed his players for

Time Magazine: Super Bowl's Super Coach

Chuck Noll was named the fourteenth head coach in Steelers history in 1969, and manned the sidelines until 1991. He led the team to four Super Bowls wins. Read more about his career on this site.

Access this Web site from http://www.myreportlinks.com

the very first time. "You could have heard a pin drop in the room," said Steelers linebacker Andy Russell. "Here was the man who could enlighten us, tell us what was wrong with us, give us new hope...."[5]

The Steelers had gone 2–11–1 the previous season. They had lacked discipline and played sloppily. Noll, a former linebacker and offensive lineman in the 1950s, knew all of Pittsburgh's problems and how to fix them. After all, he had learned the game from such coaching legends as Paul Brown and Don Shula. Noll was low-key and cerebral—a brilliant, patient teacher. Said Russell, "It was not uncommon for Chuck to stay

The Masterminds

late after a hot afternoon practice at training camp to teach techniques to some bright-eyed rookie who Chuck knew he was going to have to cut the very next day."[6]

Pittsburgh finished with its worst record ever in 1969 (1–13). But to Noll, that was almost irrelevant. His players were learning proper techniques and becoming more disciplined. Noll also

▲ Steelers broadcaster Myron Cope receives a game ball from team president Art Rooney III.

possessed a great eye for talent, and throughout the early 1970s the Steelers drafted one future star after another. In 1972, it started coming together, as Noll's well-oiled machine produced an 11–3 record. Super Bowl triumphs followed in January of 1975, 1976, 1979, and 1980.

In 23 seasons as Pittsburgh's coach, Noll went 209–156–1—including 16–8 in the postseason. Nine times he won the AFC Central Division. Through 2006, he was the only coach in NFL history to win four Super Bowl titles.

Myron Cope

Little Myron Cope stood just five feet four inches. He spoke with a nasal voice and chatted in Yiddish on occasion. Who knew he would become one of the giants of Steelers football?

Cope started out as a print journalist. His profile of broadcaster Howard Cosell for *Sports Illustrated* in 1967 is considered one of the finest articles ever written for that magazine. In the late 1960s, Cope enchanted Pittsburgh radio listeners with his sports talk show. In 1970, the Steelers hired him as their radio color commentator.

"I can remember when I was a kid listening to Myron," recalled James Farrelly of Hanover, Pennsylvania. "I could not stand that voice. How could the team hire this screeching, howling fanatic? But in the ripeness of time, I began to realize what Bill Cowher knows—that Myron is

Pittsburgh—gritty, hardworking, and determined to rise to the top of whatever challenge presents itself."[7]

While a fair and well-informed broadcaster, Cope brought color and excitement to every game. He popularized such nicknames as the "Steel Curtain" defense and the "Immaculate Reception." He expressed his emotions in Yiddish with such words as *feh* and *yoi*—and sometimes "double *yoi*." In 1975, he urged fans to wave yellow dishtowels at the upcoming playoff game, thus starting the tradition of the "Terrible Towels."

On this online pictorial called *Life:* **Classic Pictures Football,** you will find a photo from a Pittsburgh Steelers game in 1960. Browse the rest of this photo gallery to view images from other NFL games from this period.

Cope missed only one Steelers broadcast in thirty-five years—when his wife died in 1994. In 2005, he became the first football broadcaster inducted into the National Radio Hall of Fame.

Bill Cowher

In the hyper-competitive NFL, head coaches are lucky to last three years with one team. Some just hope to make it through the season. In franchise history for example, the Cardinals have employed thirty-five head coaches. But that is not how the Steelers operate. Owned by the Rooney family since 1933, Pittsburgh's NFL team employed only two head coaches from 1970 to 2007—Chuck Noll and Bill Cowher.

In high school, Cowher starred in football in Crafton, Pennsylvania, a suburb of Pittsburgh. After a five-year stint as a linebacker in the NFL, he served as an able assistant coach with Cleveland and Kansas City. In 1992, the Steelers pulled a shocker when they hired Cowher to replace Noll. After all, he was only thirty-four years old.

Cowher went 11–5 that fall, his first of six straight winning seasons. After consecutive losing campaigns in 1998 and 1999, he submitted his resignation. The Steelers would not accept it. "He's our kind of guy," owner Dan Rooney said. "He's a hard worker, he's enthusiastic, he gets

The Masterminds

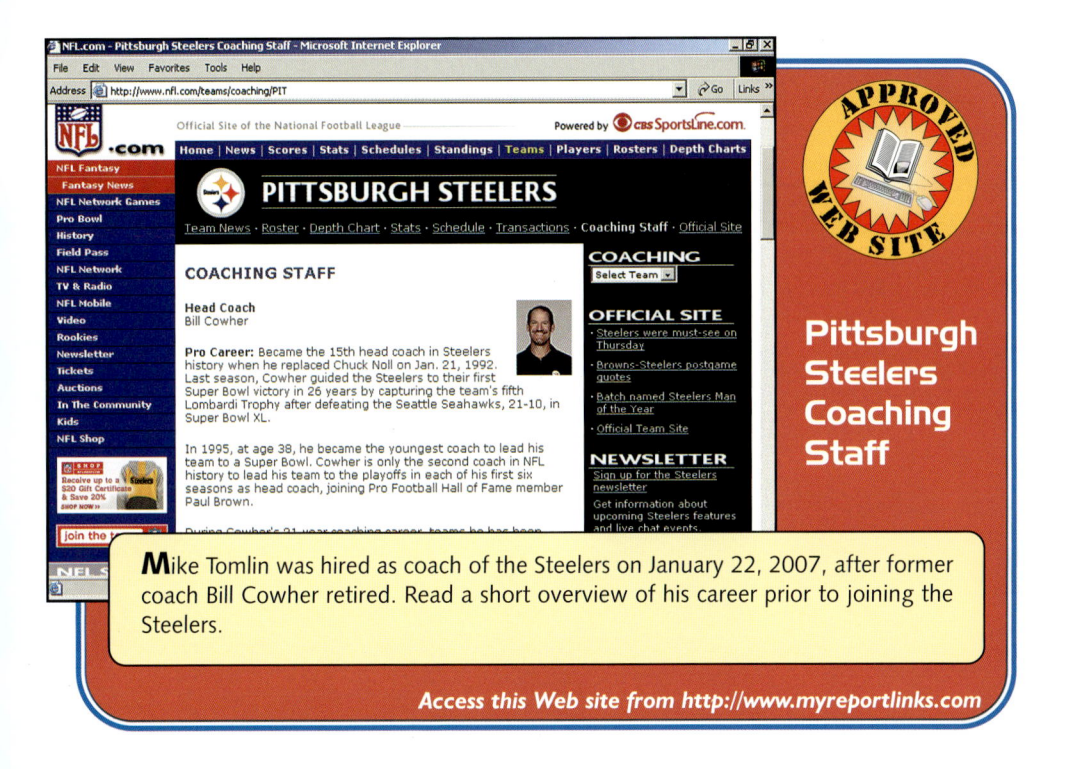

> **M**ike Tomlin was hired as coach of the Steelers on January 22, 2007, after former coach Bill Cowher retired. Read a short overview of his career prior to joining the Steelers.

Access this Web site from http://www.myreportlinks.com

along with everybody. . . . He's done what we're looking for."[8]

With his Super Bowl triumph in February 2006, Cowher completed his fourteenth season as Steelers head coach. His longevity with the same team ranked first among active NFL coaches. Along the way, he led the Steelers to eight division titles, ten playoff berths, and six appearances in the AFC Championship Game. Here is one more fact that the Steelers family can be proud of: From 1992 through 2006—the Cowher era—Pittsburgh won more games than any other NFL team.

These Steelers fans gathered on April 24, 2004, to watch the NFL Draft on the big screen at Heinz Field.

Welcome to Heinz Field

For thirty years, Steelers fans trudged to Three Rivers Stadium. They loved their ballclub, but the venue grew wearisome. The exterior was little more than a massive circle of concrete. Since the Steelers had to share the "multipurpose facility" with baseball's Pirates, the playing field was awkwardly shaped. Seats in the enclosed structure offered no views of the city. The stadium had all the charm of a parking lot.

Thankfully, Three Rivers now is a parking lot. In 2001, Pittsburgh unveiled two of the most glorious sporting venues in America: PNC Park for the Pirates and Heinz Field for the Steelers. The stadiums rest on opposite sides of the former Three Rivers Stadium, which was demolished and transformed into a parking facility.

Shaped like a horseshoe, Heinz Field offers a majestic panorama of the Pittsburgh skyline across the Ohio River. The view is just one reason why stadium aficionados rank this facility among the very best in the NFL.

Heinz Field cost $230 million to build. The city of Pittsburgh owns the stadium, but the Steelers contributed $76.5 million for its construction. The Pittsburgh-based HJ Heinz Company agreed to pay $57 million to sponsor the field. Not coincidentally, the condiments company is known for its "57 Varieties" slogan.

Architects tried to incorporate elements in Heinz Field that are distinctly Pittsburgh. Steel, for example, is the primary building material. In fact, the stadium is comprised of twelve thousand tons of structural steel. Most of the steel is silvery gray, but gold-painted "quad pods" support the upper deck. The stadium's facade, like many of Pittsburgh's landmark buildings, also incorporates stone and glass.

Inside Heinz Field

In addition to the Steelers, Heinz Field is home to the University of Pittsburgh football team, and is the venue for special area events. (On July 23, 2006, Bon Jovi headlined the Steelers World Championship Celebration Concert.) Every ticket holder is made to feel at home. Seats are exceptionally close to the field, and the upper deck does not extend into the stratosphere like in other

Welcome to Heinz Field

NFL stadiums. Seats are especially roomy and have been contoured for comfort.

Even the players' needs were taken care of. After players took a pounding on Three Rivers' artificial turf, the Steelers switched to natural bluegrass for their new field. Moreover, a heating system keeps the turf at a constant 62°F. Thus, players never have to worry about slipping or banging their knees on a frozen field.

Because the Heinz Company is famous for its condiments, and most of the stadium's seats are yellow, locals call Heinz Field the "Mustard

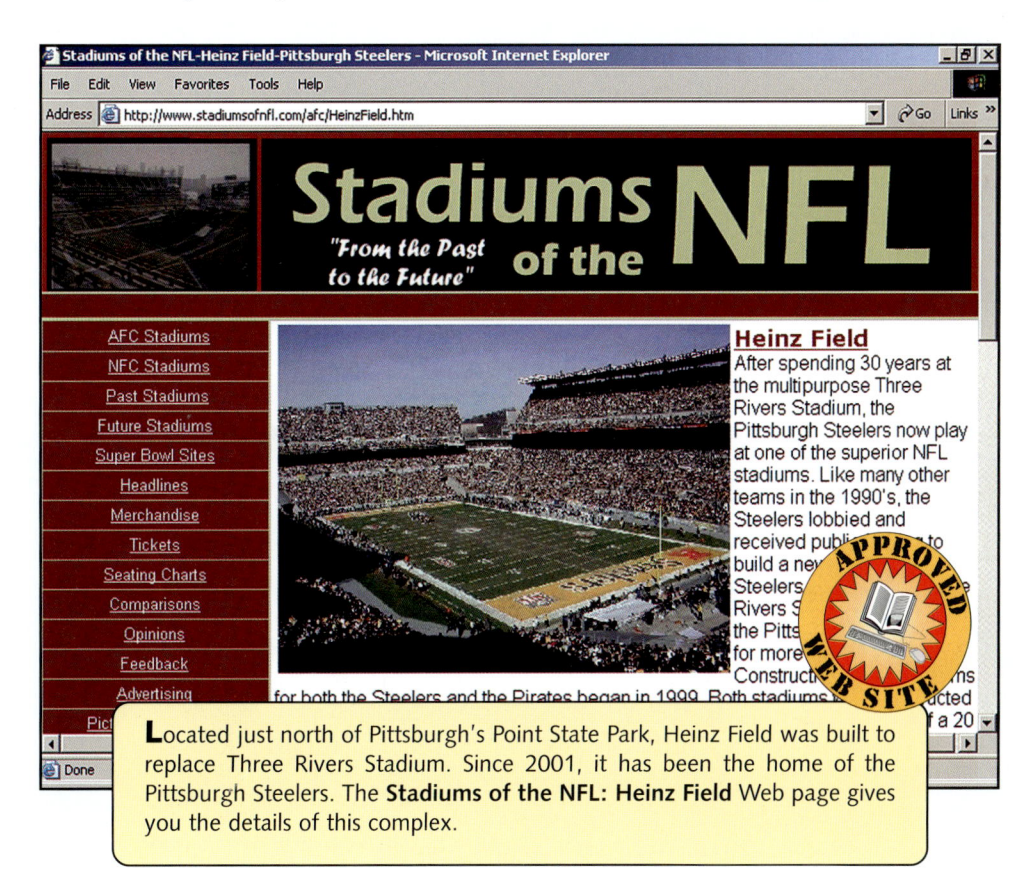

Located just north of Pittsburgh's Point State Park, Heinz Field was built to replace Three Rivers Stadium. Since 2001, it has been the home of the Pittsburgh Steelers. The **Stadiums of the NFL: Heinz Field** Web page gives you the details of this complex.

Palace." ESPN's Chris Berman refers to it as the "Big Ketchup Bottle." That is because the stadium's giant scoreboard is flanked by two enormous Heinz "ketchup bottles." When the Steelers enter the "red zone," meaning inside the opponents' 20-yard line, the neon bottles "pour" onto the screen. If the giant bottles were real, they would contain 1,664,000 ounces of ketchup.

Heinz Field seats sixty-five thousand, including approximately seven thousand at the club level. Before, during, and after games, fans gather in the two club lounges. Rising three stories, the lounges feature a wall of glass from bottom to top. They also include an enormous video wall and concession stands for specialty foods.

The Great Hall

Steelers fans who enter Heinz Field's Great Hall feel like they have gone to football heaven. Visitors can watch an inspiring film about Steelers history, or play interactive games. A Steelers "Hall of Fame" includes lockers, uniforms, and mementos of such legends as Mean Joe Greene. Fans beam with Pittsburgh pride as they walk past replicas of the Steelers' Super Bowl trophies. In another section, a multimedia exhibit made up of 334 lights and 38 speakers blast "flashbacks" to great moments in Steelers history. All the while, fans can purchase Pittsburgh delicacies from such

Welcome to Heinz Field

Get up-to-date information on the Pittsburgh Steelers when you visit this site. Multimedia features, fan forums, photo galleries, and lots of statistics are included.

Access this Web site from http://www.myreportlinks.com

local favorites as Benkovitz Fish and Quaker Steak & Lube.

➲ Tailgatin' Tuna Salad

In Pittsburgh, tailgating is more than a parking lot picnic. It is a way of life. Even in icy, frigid weather, fans arrive at Heinz Field on Sunday morning to prepare their feast. The Steelers' official Web site offers nearly a hundred entrees perfect for Heinz Field tailgating. The most intriguing include the Tailgatin' Tuna Salad, the MVP Cheeseburger Macaroni, and the Punt-n-Pass Pork Po Boys. Many tailgaters bring a sack of Primanti Brothers sandwiches to the party. These French bread babies are packed with meat, cheese, coleslaw, and even French fries.

When the feast is over, tailgaters pack up their food and head to the stadium. They make sure they bring their ticket, keys, wallet, and the most important item of all: the "Terrible Towel."

Myron Cope's Gimmick

In 1975, the Steelers sales staff invited team broadcaster Myron Cope to a meeting. They told Cope that they wanted a gimmick to promote at Pittsburgh's upcoming playoff game against Baltimore. Someone suggested that fans wear black masks to the game, but that idea was rejected.

"How about towels?" said Larry Garrett, vice president for sales. Fans could wave them maniacally in the stands.[1]

"We could call it the Terrible Towel," said Cope. "Yes, and I can go on radio and television proclaiming, The Terrible Towel is poised to strike!"[2]

Everyone in the room loved the idea. A few nights later, Cope went on the eleven o'clock news. He told fans to bring yellow or gold towels to the game, and he flung some at the anchorman and weatherman for good measure. The Steelers went on to rout Baltimore 28–10—thanks, of course, to the Terrible Towels. For that season's Super Bowl, the Steelers produced gold

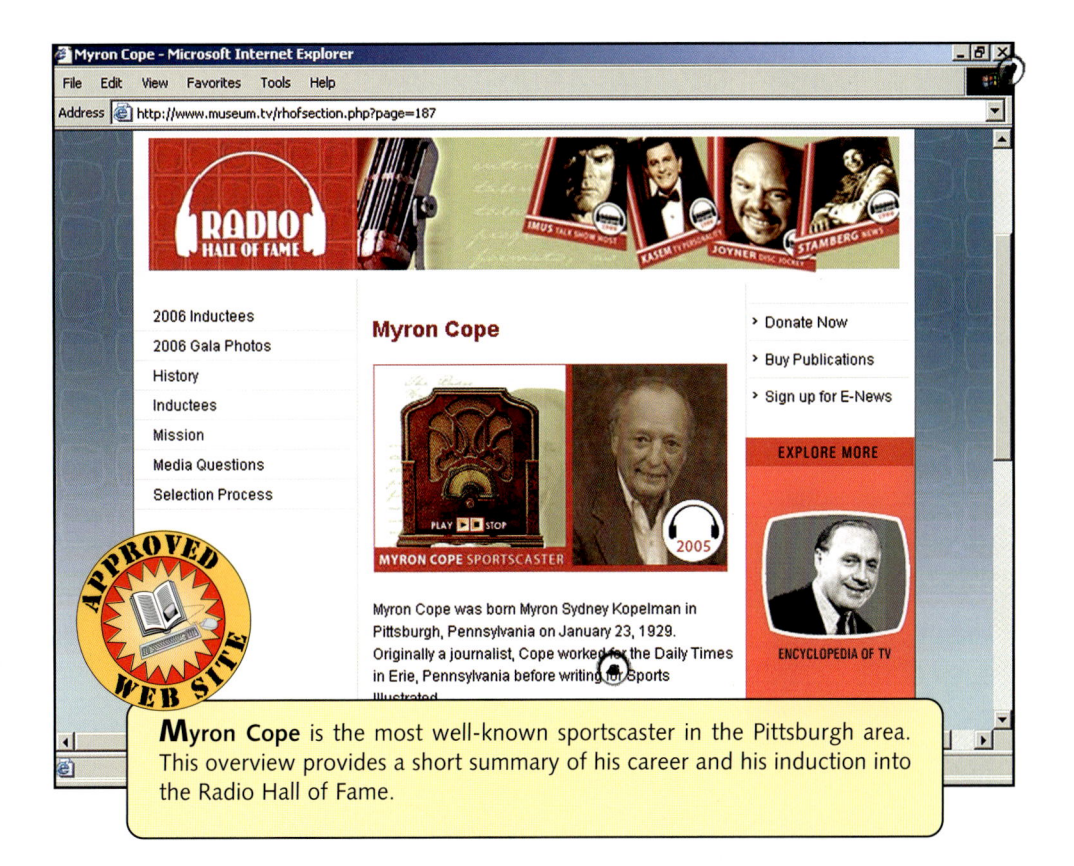

Myron Cope is the most well-known sportscaster in the Pittsburgh area. This overview provides a short summary of his career and his induction into the Radio Hall of Fame.

towels with the words "Myron Cope's Terrible Towels."

What started as a gimmick has lasted more than thirty years. In fact, for Super Bowl XL in 2006, waving Terrible Towels became a national sensation. Cope, meanwhile, turned something "terrible" into something wonderful. In 1996, he gave the rights to the Terrible Towel to the Allegheny Valley School, which cares for people with mental and physical disabilities. Proceeds from the towels have generated more than $1 million for the school.

MyReportLinks.com Books

Pittsburgh Steelers fans are known for waving their yellow and black Terrible Towels. They have been doing this since Myron Cope broadcast the idea in 1975.

Following the Steelers

As with every other NFL team, Steelers games are broadcast on the national networks: FOX, NBC, CBS, and ESPN. However, many locals hit the TV mute button and turn on the Steelers' radio broadcast team. Bill Hillgrove, who has served as the play-by-play man for a dozen years, defends the fact that he is a "homer" announcer. "When I do the Steelers [games]," Hillgrove said, "98 percent listening are rooting for them."[3] Tunç İlkin handles the analysis on the radio broadcasts. Few question the opinions of the former Steelers All-Pro offensive tackle—at least not to his face!

A horde of print journalists covers the Steelers, led by the reporters of the *Pittsburgh Post-Gazette*. The team also offers its own magazine, *Steelers Digest*, as well as its own Web site, which profiles every man on the roster, and is a one-stop source for news, stats, and multimedia fun. The site also describes how you can join the team's two official fan clubs.

Welcome to Heinz Field

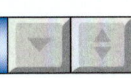

Visit **The Official Site of the Pittsburgh Steelers** for the latest information on the Pittsburgh Steelers. You can find news, photos, statistics, articles, player biographies, and much more.

EDITOR'S CHOICE

For ten dollars a year, children ages seven to twelve can join the Steelers Kids Club. Members receive a dozen goodies, such as a mini football and a helmet decal. Members of the Official Pittsburgh Steelers Fan Club can sign up for the Black Level ($30 annually) or Gold Level ($75). Those who choose Gold receive twenty-two gifts, including a free visit to the Steelers' training camp. After Pittsburgh's Super Bowl championship, a huge number of fans went for the Gold in 2006.

Byron "Whizzer" White was a star running back for the Pittsburgh Pirates in 1938. He left football for a legal career and eventually became an associate justice on the U.S. Supreme Court.

The Heroes

When *The Sporting News* selected its one hundred greatest football players of the twentieth century, Pittsburgh Steelers peppered the list. Three lined up behind each other in the Pittsburgh backfield: center Mike Webster, quarterback Terry Bradshaw, and running back Franco Harris. Four other *TSN* selections starred on defense for the Steelers: linebackers Jack Lambert and Jack Ham, and cornerbacks Mel Blount and Rod Woodson. This chapter profiles fifteen larger-than-life legends who wore the gold and black.

Byron "Whizzer" White

Desperate for fans in 1938, Pittsburgh paid what was then an enormous $15,000 salary to a rookie wunderkind from the University of Colorado. Denver sportswriter Leonard Kahn had nicknamed

Byron White "Whizzer" because "he seemed to whiz by people."[1]

As an All-American selection in 1937, White had led the nation in rushing with 1,121 yards. More impressively, he averaged an amazing 8.4 yards per carry. He also starred on defense, and he boomed a punt 83 yards. For the Colorado baseball team, he batted .400—and he excelled on the school basketball squad. In the classroom, he earned a Rhodes Scholarship to Oxford University in England.

White captivated the nation, and the Pittsburgh Pirates promoted him heavily. Though he struggled to find running room with the woeful Pirates, Whizzer led the NFL in rushing as a rookie with 567 yards. In one late-season game, he romped for 133 yards, including 79 on one play.

White played just two more seasons in the NFL, both with the Detroit Lions. After graduating first in his class at Yale Law School, he began a highly esteemed law career. From 1962 to 1993, he served as an associate justice on the U.S. Supreme Court.

Ernie Stautner

Baltimore Colts offensive lineman Jim Parker usually overpowered his opponents. However, he was no match for Steelers defensive lineman Ernie "The Horse" Stautner. "That man ain't human,"

Ernie "The Horse" Stautner was one of the most dominant defensive linemen of the 1950s and early 1960s. This image was taken in 1963 when he served as a player-coach.

claimed Parker. "He's too strong to be human. . . . [He] used to stick his head in my belly and drive me into the backfield so hard that, when I picked myself up and looked around, there was a path chopped through the field like a farmer had run a plow over it."[2]

A native of Bavaria, Stautner immigrated to Albany, New York, at age three. He served in the U.S. Marine Corps before joining the NFL. In fourteen seasons with the Steelers, he missed only six games. Nine times he was named to the Pro Bowl.

Parker was just one of many opponents who Stautner drove backward. When The Horse retired in 1963, he ranked as the NFL career leader in safeties with 3. His 23 recovered fumbles ranked third on the league's all-time list. To this day, Stautner's No. 70 is the only number retired by the Pittsburgh Steelers.

Mean Joe Greene

Steelers linebacker Andy Russell remembered Joe Greene's very first practice with the Steelers in 1969. "Greene just took [Steelers center Ray] Mansfield and destroyed him," Russell said. "Just picked him up and threw him away. We were all in shock. Just in shock. Then he just destroyed the running back. Bruce Van Dyke was next. . . . Joe destroyed him, and I'm like, 'Oh my gosh, we've got a player.'"[3]

Though unheralded out of North Texas State, Greene dominated immediately. The rookie defensive tackle was big (six feet four inches, 275 pounds), powerful, quick, and fast. In addition,

Greene Brought Back by Steelers

Defensive tackle Joe Greene was drafted by the Pittsburgh Steelers, playing for the team his entire career. This article discusses how Bill Cowher brought him back to coach.

Access this Web site from http://www.myreportlinks.com

The Heroes

Mean Joe had a temper that scared opponents and made even his teammates a little uncomfortable. But he was just what the Steelers needed. He became the cornerstone of the defense that helped produce four Super Bowl titles.

In 1974, Greene began to line up at a sharp angle between the guard and center. The tactic disrupted the opposing team's blocking assignments. That year, Greene won his second NFL Defensive Player of the Year Award. From 1969 to 1979, he earned all-conference recognition every season.

Late in his career, Greene was one of the most revered figures in sports. Only in a famous Coca-Cola commercial did he seem to show America his soft side. He smiled at a young fan who had offered Greene his Coke, and tossed the kid his jersey. The boy, and America, watched in awe.

Jack Ham

When you watch Jack Ham on film, said former Steelers assistant coach George Perles, "you feel like standing up and applauding."[4] Ham was a coach's favorite kind of player—one who used his wits to outsmart the opposition.

Ham graduated in 1971 from Penn State, known as "Linebacker U." Well schooled in that craft by Penn State coach Joe Paterno, Ham earned the starting left linebacker job as a rookie. He immediately excelled with his speed and

MyReportLinks.com Books

> Joe Greene was one of the best defensive linemen of his time. This **Joe Greene** player page for the tackler has his games played stats and a short summary of his career.

intelligence. Ham anticipated plays before they developed, and reacted instantly. He stuffed fullbacks at the line of scrimmage, and he derailed halfbacks on outside sweeps. He was about as likely to sack a quarterback as pick off his pass. For his career, he logged 25 1/2 sacks and 32 interceptions.

Said Houston Oilers head coach Bum Phillips: "In a way, he made it easy for us to come up with a game plan. We'd just run the other way. We wanted no part of him."[5]

The Heroes

Coaches around the NFL recognized Ham's contributions. He was named to eight straight Pro Bowls, and he was in inducted into the Pro Football Hall of Fame. He is universally regarded as one of the smartest defensive players in the history of football.

Franco Harris

When in doubt, give it to Franco. Such was the thought in Pittsburgh during Franco Harris's long

▲ Steelers running back Franco Harris breaks the tackle of Jimmy Ware of the Oakland Raiders on his way to the end zone. This image is from the legendary play known as the Immaculate Reception.

and glorious career. With a complete package of skills, Harris reigned as the most dependable running back in the NFL for more than a decade.

At 225 pounds, Harris could bull through defenders. Yet he was quick and shifty for his size, allowing him to cut through holes. When he found daylight, he had the speed to blast downfield.

As a rookie in 1972, Harris rushed for 1,055 yards while averaging 5.6 yards per carry. He was cheered on by his fellow Italian fans, known as "Franco's Italian Army." After dipping to 698 yards in 1973, Harris compiled six consecutive 1,000-yard seasons. In 1983, he set an NFL record at the time with his eighth career 1,000-yard campaign. His finest hour came in Super Bowl IX, when he ran for 158 yards to earn MVP honors.

When he finally retired in 1984, Harris had rushed for 12,120 yards—third most in NFL history at the time. Harris was named to nine Pro Bowls and inducted into the Pro Football Hall of Fame.

Jack Lambert

Gerry Myers, Jack Lambert's football coach at Crestwood High School in Ohio, remembered his star player: "I can close my eyes now and see him hitting the split end from Streetsboro. Knocked his helmet and one shoe off."[6]

Of the many standouts on the Steel Curtain defense, Lambert may have been the greatest of

▲ *Jack Lambert (No. 58) drags down Bengals running back Archie Griffin. Jack Ham is also in on the tackle.*

all. In fact, the middle linebacker reigned as team captain for eight straight seasons.

Lambert was quick and agile, and he hit like a Mack truck. Coaches raved about his intelligence and intensity. A quarterback's knees would turn to jelly when he caught a glimpse of Lambert's face: his menacing sneer, his crazed eyes, and his three missing front teeth. "It's what Attila must've looked like while he was sacking a village," wrote *Sports Illustrated's* Paul Zimmerman, "or the way a Viking chieftain was with his blood lust up."[7]

Lambert was voted NFL Defensive Rookie of the Year in 1974, and he was named All-Pro eight times. In 1976, he earned the NFL Defensive Player of the Year Award. Many have called him the greatest linebacker to ever play the game.

Mel Blount

As a starting cornerback in 1972, Mel Blount achieved a feat unheard of in pro football. He did not allow his opposing receivers to score a single touchdown all season. "I never saw a cornerback like him," said teammate Jack Ham. "He was the most incredible athlete I have ever seen. With Mel, you could take one wide receiver and just write him off. He could handle anybody in the league."[8]

Blount had the speed and quickness to stick with the speediest of receivers. His exceptional

The Heroes

height (six feet three inches) and long arms allowed him to snatch or deflect high passes. In addition, he had the strength of a linebacker. Blount's favorite technique was the bump-and-run. He bashed receivers as soon as they crossed the line of scrimmage, disrupting their routes.

In fourteen seasons with the Steelers, Blount amassed 57 interceptions. In 1975, he picked off 11 passes and was named NFL Defensive Player of the Year by the Associated Press. When *The*

▲ *Mel Blount is considered by many to be one of the best defensive backs of all time. In this photo, Ed Newman of the Dolphins can only watch from the ground as Blount returns a fumble.*

Sporting News picked its one hundred greatest players of the twentieth century, Blount ranked thirty-sixth on the list. He was inducted into the Pro Football Hall of Fame in 1989.

Terry Bradshaw

In 1970, quarterback Terry Bradshaw entered the NFL with a rocket arm and unfair expectations. Through 1973, the country boy from Louisiana Tech was abused as much by fans as by opposing pass rushers. "I had people call me a dummy and a hick," Bradshaw wrote. "I had a lady stop me outside the stadium and tell me I stunk. I heard the people cheer when I got hurt."[9]

During the 1974 season, Bradshaw's supporting cast improved—and all of a sudden everyone loved Bradshaw. Though he played in only eight regular-season games during that season, Bradshaw shone brightly in the playoffs. His ability to rifle balls deep downfield helped stretch and soften opposing defenses. From 1974 to 1979, he led Pittsburgh to four Super Bowl titles.

The fun-loving QB rose to the occasion in big games. In four Super Bowls, he passed for 932 yards and 9 touchdowns. Bradshaw earned MVP honors in Super Bowl XIII and XIV, as the Steelers topped 30 points in each game. In 1978, he fired 28 touchdown passes during the regular season

▲ *In this Super Bowl XIII action, Terry Bradshaw is turning to hand off to Steelers running back Rocky Bleier.*

and was named NFL MVP by the Associated Press.

At the conclusion of his Hall of Fame career in 1983, Bradshaw signed a broadcasting contract with CBS. He has been a television fixture on NFL Sundays ever since.

Lynn Swann

Lynn Swann literally danced his way to NFL glory. From age four until his senior year of high school, Swann took various dance lessons—including ballet. As an NFL receiver, he dazzled the nation with his balletic grace.

His career-defining play came in Super Bowl X against Dallas. On a deep pass by Terry Bradshaw, Swann dove for the ball, tipped it up, twisted in midair, and caught it while lying on the ground. He finished the game with 4 catches and a whopping 161 yards, earning the Super Bowl MVP Award.

In addition to his amazing grace, Swann was exceptionally fast and athletic. In high school, he set a school record in the long jump. He was also fearless. As a rookie in 1974, he called only 3 fair catches in 41 punt returns. That mental toughness allowed him to rise for catches in the middle of the field, knowing that defenders were ready to abuse his slender frame.

Swann earned All-Pro honors in 1975, 1977, and 1978. Though his 5,462 receiving yards were not extraordinary, he earned "style points" in the eyes of Hall of Fame voters. In 2001, he earned induction. Five years later, he strove for even greater glory, running for governor in Pennsylvania.

L. C. Greenwood

His name was Greenwood, but L. C. was known for a wide range of colors. He wore distinctive gold shoes, and he left opponents black and blue—and

▲ *Opposing quarterbacks feared Pittsburgh defensive end L. C. Greenwood (shown here).*

sometimes bloody red. In 1991, he was named to the Super Bowl Silver Anniversary Team.

Greenwood got his start in 1969, when Pittsburgh drafted him down in the tenth round. In 1971, he won the starting job at left defensive end—and kept it for another ten years. Greenwood played a prominent role in the Steel Curtain defense due largely to his massive six-foot six-inch frame. He led Pittsburgh in sacks in four seasons and amassed 73.5 in his career. From 1973 to 1979, he made the Pro Bowl six times.

Some of Greenwood's best performances came on the big stage. In Super Bowl IX against the Minnesota Vikings, he swatted down 3 passes. A year later, he sacked Dallas quarterback Roger Staubach 3 times. But more than anything else, Greenwood was famous for his gold shoes.

In 1973, Greenwood was instructed to wear high-top shoes because of his injured ankles. High-tops were not not in vogue at the time, and the equipment manager could find only an ugly pair of black ones. Jokingly, Greenwood asked that they be painted gold. The manager obliged, and Greenwood wore the luminous high-tops for the rest of his career.

John Stallworth

It is not surprising that nearly every team overlooked receiver John Stallworth in the 1974 NFL Draft. He had played in obscurity at Alabama

The Heroes

A&M, and his official time in the 40-yard dash was an unimpressive 4.8 seconds. The slow time, however, was due to a hip injury. Thus, the Steelers got a steal in the fourth round of the draft.

That season, Pittsburgh premiered two rookie receivers who would one day be enshrined in the Pro Football Hall of Fame: Lynn Swann and Stallworth. Swann made the fancier catches, but

▲ *Leaping into the air, John Stallworth pulls down a touchdown reception during the first quarter of Super Bowl XIII.*

Stallworth was the workhorse. He ran crisp routes and caught everything he could reach. "It just came natural," he explained. "I would reach out to catch the ball, and it would just stick. It's always been a God-given talent that I possess."[10]

Stallworth got better with age, earning his four Pro Bowl selections in 1979, 1982, 1983, and 1984. In his fourteen-year career, all with Pittsburgh, he smashed team records for receptions (537), yards receiving (8,723), and TD catches (63).

Upon his retirement, Stallworth held seven Super Bowl records. His heroics on the big stage are legendary. In Super Bowl XIII, he tallied 75- and 28-yard touchdown grabs in the first half. And a year later, he raced 73 yards for the winning touchdown. He joined Swann in the Hall of Fame in 2002.

Mike Webster

Late in a 1988 game, in a blowout loss to Phoenix, Steelers coach Bill Cowher replaced all of his offensive starters—except one. Veteran center Mike Webster remained in the game. His body was covered with dirt, grass, and bloodstains. His jersey was torn and his helmet was damaged. But he did not leave the field.

"Men, one thing you can never do in this league is quit," Webster said to his teammates during a fourth-quarter time-out that game. "You

The Heroes

have to finish every play and finish every game. We're going to take this ball and go down the field."[11]

A fifth-round pick in 1974, Webster was not good enough to start as a rookie. He persevered, however, eventually becoming the strongest man on the team. He cracked the starting lineup late in 1975 and never looked back. Through 1986, he made 150 consecutive starts.

Steelers stalwart center Mike Webster played for the team for fifteen years. This image was from the 1988 season.

Pittsburgh's "iron man" set team records for most seasons (15) and games (220). He then played two more years with Kansas City. Clearly one of the greatest centers ever, Webster was named All-Pro seven times. In 1997, he was inducted into the Pro Football Hall of Fame.

Rod Woodson

In 1998, Keyshawn Johnson was a young, hot-shot receiver for the New York Jets. In September, he squared off against Baltimore Ravens cornerback Rod Woodson, an "old man" of thirty-three. Woodson humbled Johnson with 2 interceptions, one of which he returned 60 yards for a touchdown.

"If his skills have eroded quite a bit, I don't know what he looked like in his prime," Johnson mused. "He must have been Superman."[12]

For seventeen NFL seasons—the first ten with Pittsburgh—Woodson shut down opposing wide receivers. He was so fast and athletic that he once qualified for the Olympic trials in the 110-meter hurdles. In addition, said Johnson, "He probably is the smartest I have played against. The rest of them [opposing cornerbacks] never showed stuff like he did."[13]

In his career, Woodson picked off 71 passes. His 1,483 interception return yards set an NFL record, as did his 12 interceptions returned for touchdowns. Woodson was named to 11 Pro Bowls, including seven in a row with the Steelers beginning in 1989. In 1995, he became the first NFL player to have reconstructive knee surgery and return the same season.

Woodson was named Associated Press Defensive Player of the Year in 1993, and he made

▲ *Cornerback and safety Rod Woodson was one of the best players of his time, particularly during the 1990s. After his playing days were over, Woodson became a television commentator.*

the NFL All-Decade Team for the 1990s. In 2001, *USA Today* named Woodson the greatest NFL defensive player on the newspaper's twentieth anniversary team.

Jerome Bettis

Because of the punishment they absorb, running backs last, on average, two-and-a-half years in the NFL. Jerome Bettis played thirteen.

At five feet eleven inches, 255 pounds, "The Bus" rode over defensive tackles and dragged linebackers downfield. However, Bettis's 3,479 career carries took their toll. His knees, ankles, shoulders, head, neck, hip—they all throbbed in pain. In 2005, he explained why The Bus was still in service. "I'm going to hurt Monday," he said. "I'm probably going to hurt Tuesday. You know what? Wednesday, I'm probably not going to feel great. But Thursday, I'm going to feel fine. Friday, I'll be OK. Saturday, I get to rest. And Sunday, I'm going to beat your head in again."[14]

Drafted out of Notre Dame in 1993, Bettis rushed for 1,429 yards as a rookie with the Los Angeles Rams. Upon joining Pittsburgh in 1996, he rumbled for six straight one thousand-yard seasons—with a high of 1,665 in 1997. Five times he earned a trip to the Pro Bowl.

The Heroes

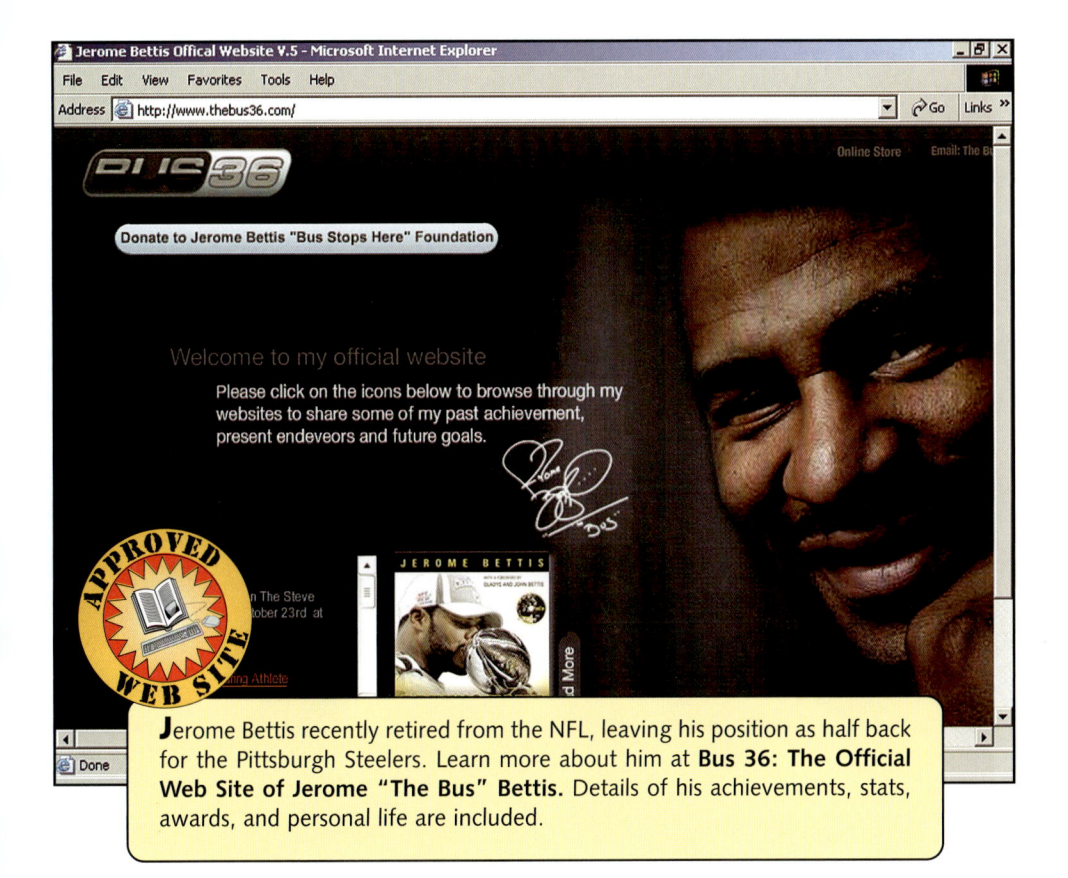

Jerome Bettis recently retired from the NFL, leaving his position as half back for the Pittsburgh Steelers. Learn more about him at **Bus 36: The Official Web Site of Jerome "The Bus" Bettis.** Details of his achievements, stats, awards, and personal life are included.

All the while, Bettis won over hearts in Pittsburgh. His "The Bus Stops Here" Foundation has supported underprivileged children. For years he hosted the *The Jerome Bettis Show*—a local sports and entertainment television program. In 2005, he became the first recipient of the Pro Football Writers of America's award for media cooperation.

Despite his retirement, fans will still get to watch The Bus every football Sunday. In 2006, he signed to serve as a studio commentator for NBC's *Football Night in America*.

▲ Hines Ward dives over Eagles safety Brian Dawkins to score a touchdown. This game took place on November 7, 2004.

Hines Ward

Hines Ward won the MVP Award in Super Bowl XL, and the world is better off for it.

Ward had grown up in Atlanta as a biracial child—half African American, half Korean. "I was a lost child," he said. "I wasn't accepted in the black community because I was Korean, and I wasn't accepted in the Korean community because I was black."[15]

After the Super Bowl, Ward was invited to tour South Korea, a nation that is home to roughly five thousand Amerasians. These biracial people are shunned in their country; nearly half of Amerasian adults are unemployed or have to work odd jobs to get by. During his highly publicized trip, Ward met South Korea's president and served as an inspirational role model. "That guy has no idea how much good he's doing," said Janet Mintzer, president of an American organization that supports mixed-race children in South Korea.[16]

Among Steelers fans, Ward had been a hero for eight seasons. Each year from 2001 through 2004, he topped a thousand yards in receiving yards and made the Pro Bowl. In 2005, he set the Steelers record for most career receptions. His 123 yards in that season's Super Bowl earned him the game's top honors. Two months later, Ward was off to the Far East, ready to serve a higher calling.

| Back | Forward | Stop | Review | Home | Explore | Favorites | History |

Report Links

The Internet sites described below can be accessed at http://www.myreportlinks.com

▶ **The Official Site of the Pittsburgh Steelers**
Editor's Choice Browse the official Web site of the Pittsburgh Steelers.

▶ **Official Site of the National Football League**
Editor's Choice Get the latest news from the official Web site of the NFL.

▶ **Pro Football Hall of Fame**
Editor's Choice This is the online home and official Web site of the Pro Football Hall of Fame.

▶ **Steelers/NFL**
Editor's Choice This *Pittsburgh Post-Gazette* Web site is an online home for Steelers information.

▶ **SuperBowl.com**
Editor's Choice Learn about the history of the Super Bowl on this Web site.

▶ **The Story Behind the Pittsburgh Steelers Logo**
Editor's Choice This American Iron and Steel Institute news release explains the Steelers logo.

▶ **Arthur J. Rooney 1901–1988**
Read about the life and times of Steelers owner and founder, Art Rooney.

▶ **"Art Rooney II Replaces Father as Steelers President"**
This newspaper article covers the passing of the Steelers torch from one Rooney to another.

▶ **Big Ben 7: Welcome to the Official Website of Super Bowl Champion Ben Roethlisberger**
This is the official Web site of Steelers QB Ben Roethlisberger.

▶ **Bus 36: The Official Web Site of Jerome "The Bus" Bettis**
This is the official Web site for running back Jerome Bettis.

▶ **Greene Brought Back by Steelers**
This CBC Sports article announces Mean Joe Greene's return to the Steelers organization.

▶ **Joe Greene**
The Pro Football Hall of Fame has posted this profile of Joe Greene.

▶ **John Henry Johnson**
A short biography and a few pictures of John Henry Johnson are available on this Web site.

▶ **Johnny Unitas**
Find out more about Johnny Unitas from this official Web site.

▶ ***Life* Classic Pictures: Football**
View classic pictures of the NFL from *Life* magazine.

Visit "My Toolkit" at www.myreportlinks.com for tips on using the Internet.

MyReportLinks.com Books

Tools Search Notes Discuss

Report Links

The Internet sites described below can be accessed at
http://www.myreportlinks.com

▶**Myron Cope**
This Museum of Broadcast Communications Web article highlights sportscaster Myron Cope.

▶**Pigskin Physics and the Immaculate Reception**
Find out if physics played a role in the Immaculate Reception.

▶**Pittsburgh Steelers Clubhouse**
Visit this ESPN site for the Pittsburgh Steelers.

▶**Pittsburgh Steelers Coaching Staff**
For biographical information on head coach Mike Tomlin and his assistants, visit this site.

▶**Pittsburgh Steelers (1933–Present)**
This time line covers the most important highlights in Steelers history.

▶**The Pittsburgh Steelers Teams From the Past**
This Web site takes you on a tour of Steelers teams from the 1930s to the 1960s.

▶**President Welcomes Super Bowl Champion Pittsburgh Steelers to the White House**
Learn about the Steelers' trip to the White House.

▶**Professional Football Researchers Association: Sutherland**
The Professional Football Researchers Association summarizes the career of Jock Sutherland.

▶**Stadiums of the NFL: Heinz Field**
This site has facts, figures, and photos of the Heinz Field.

▶**Steelers' Defense Stuns Vikings, 16–6**
This *Washington Post* article takes a look at Super Bowl IX.

▶**Steelers Fever**
Keep track of the Steelers by visiting this fan Web site.

▶**Super Bowl XL: Pittsburgh 21, Seattle 10**
This SuperBowl.com wire report provides an overview of the game in Detroit.

▶**Super Bowl Reflections: Terry Bradshaw**
This article appeared in the program for Super Bowl XXXIII.

▶***Time* Magazine: Super Bowl's Super Coach**
This is a short biography of Chuck Noll.

▶**Welcome to the Official Lynn Swann Web Site!**
This is the official Web site for former football player Lynn Swann.

Any comments? Contact us: comments@myreportlinks.com

Career

GREAT HEAD COACHES*	SEA	W	L	T	PCT
Jock Sutherland	1946–47	13	9	1	.587
Buddy Parker	1957–68	51	47	6	.519
Chuck Noll	1969–91	193	148	1	.566
Bill Cowher	1992–2006	149	90	1	.623

*Only includes seasons with Steelers

QUARTERBACKS	Y	G	ATT	COMP	YDS	TD
Terry Bradshaw	14	168	3,901	2,025	27,989	212
Bobby Layne	15	173	3,700	1,814	26,768	196
Neil O'Donnell	13	123	3,229	1,865	21,690	120
Ben Roethlisberger	3	42	1,032	644	8,519	52
Kordell Stewart	11	126	2,358	1,316	14,746	77

RUNNING BACKS	Y	G	ATT	YDS	AVG	TD
Jerome Bettis	13	192	3,479	13,662	3.9	91
Franco Harris	13	173	2,949	12,120	4.1	91
John Henry Johnson	13	136	1,571	6,803	4.3	48
Willie Parker	3	39	624	2,882	4.6	17

Stats

WIDE RECEIVERS	Y	G	REC	YDS	AVG	TD
Buddy Dial	8	98	261	5,436	20.8	44
Louis Lipps	9	110	359	6,019	16.8	39
John Stallworth	14	165	537	8,723	16.2	63
Lynn Swann	9	116	336	5,462	16.3	51
Hines Ward	9	141	648	8,005	12.4	58

DEFENSIVE PLAYERS	Y	G	PRO BOWLS	INT
Mel Blount	14	200	5	57
Joe Greene	13	181	10	1
Jack Ham	12	162	8	32
Jack Lambert	11	146	9	28
Greg Lloyd	11	122	5	11
Joey Porter	8	122	3	10
Rod Woodson	17	⬢	11	71

Y=Years G=Games ATT=Attempts YDS=Yards AVG=Average TD=Touch Downs
COMP=Completions INT=Interceptions REC=Receptions PCT=Winning Percentage
SEA=Seasons W=Wins

Glossary

agile—Able to move quickly and with grace.

amassed—Accumulated or collected.

blitz—A defensive tactic used in football in which the defense sends more players than the offense can handle in an effort to tackle the opponent's quarterback or prevent him from completing a pass.

center—The football player who has the middle position in the line when starting a play. He snaps the ball between his legs to the quarterback.

consecutive—One after the other.

draft—The selection of college and foreign players each year by NFL teams. Normally the teams with the worst records get to choose first.

franchise—A team that has membership in a professional sports league.

fumble—To lose hold of the football while running with it.

interception—When a defensive player makes an interception he catches an errant pass from the quarterback. The defensive player gains control of the ball for his team.

ligaments—Tissues that connect the joints of the bones or support of an organ.

pigskin—Another word for a football.

quarterback—In football, the quarterback usually stands behind the center and calls all the signals. He directs the play when his team is in possession of the ball.

revenue—Total profit made.

romp—An easy win.

rookie—A player in his first year with a major professional sport.

roster—List of all players on a team.

rout—To defeat.

running back—The football player who carries the ball during an offensive play.

rush—To carry the football closer to the end zone.

safety—In football, a position in the defensive backfield. There are normally two safeties, a free safety and a strong safety. They are the last line of defense. Also, a play in football that occurs when quarterback is sacked in his team's own end zone. The defensive team earns two points, and the offensive team then has to punt the ball away.

stellar—Outstanding.

tenacious—Strong and persistent.

Chapter Notes

Chapter 1. Riding "The Bus" to the Super Bowl

1. Jarrett Bell, "'Bus' gets Motor City revved up for XL game," *USA Today*, February 2, 2006, <http://www.usatoday.com/sports/football/nfl/steelers/2006-02-02-bettis-cover_x.htm> (April 21, 2006).

2. Alan Robinson (Associated Press), "Next Bus stop for Steelers: the Super Bowl," *Indiana Daily Student,* January 23, 2006, <http://www.idsnews.com/news/story.php?id=33411> (April 21, 2006).

3. Wayne Drehs, "Homecoming brings memories for Bettis family," *ESPN.com,* January 29, 2006, <http://sports.espn.go.com/nfl/playoffs05/news/story?id=2310876> (April 21, 2006).

4. Greg Garber, "Bettis drives off in style," *ESPN.com,* February 6, 2006, <http://sports.espn.go.com/nfl/playoffs05/news/story?id=2320642> (April 23, 2006).

5. Associated Press, "Update: Kilpatrick presents Bettis with key to the city," *The Detroit News,* January 31, 2006, <http://www.detnews.com/apps/pbcs.dll/article?AID=/20060131/SPORTS0106/601310443> (April 23, 2006).

6. Wayne Drehs, "Homecoming brings memories for Bettis family," *ESPN.com,* January 29, 2006, <http://sports.espn.go.com/nfl/playoffs05/news/story?id=2310876> (April 26, 2006).

7. Jarrett Bell, "'Bus' gets Motor City revved up for XL game," *USA Today,* February 2, 2006, <http://www.usatoday.com/sports/football/nfl/steelers/2006-02-02-bettis-cover_x.htm> (April 26, 2006).

8. Greg Garber, "Bettis drives off in style," *ESPN.com,* February 6, 2006, <http://sports.espn.go.com/nfl/playoffs05/news/story?id=2320642> (April 26, 2006).

9. Ibid.

10. Chuck Johnson, "Decorated 'Bus' says he's reached end of line," *USA Today,* February 6, 2006, <http://www.usatoday.com/sports/football/nfl/steelers/2006-02-06-bettis_x.htm> (April 26, 2006).

Chapter 2. Four Decades of Futility

1. "Arthur J. Rooney in 1983," *UK Black and Gold,* n.d., <http://www.pittsburghsteelers.co.uk/steelers/rooneys/page4.htm> (July 9, 2006).

Chapter Notes

2. Ibid.

3. Bill Chastain, *Steel Dynasty: The Team That Changed the NFL* (Chicago: Triumph Books, 2005), p. 5.

4. Jim O'Brien, *Steelers Forever: They Played and Stayed in Pittsburgh* (Pittsburgh: James P. O'Brien Publishing, 2002), p. 408.

Chapter 3. Stainless Steel Trophies

1. "Arthur J. Rooney in 1983," *UK Black and Gold*, n.d., <http://www.pittsburghsteelers.co.uk/steelers/rooneys/page4.htm> (July 13, 2006).

2. Bill Chastain, *Steel Dynasty: The Team That Changed the NFL* (Chicago: Triumph Books, 2005), p. 31.

3. "The Steelers Get Lucky," *Rodale,* n.d., <http://64.233.167.104/search?q=cache:YC908yx5sM8J:images.rodale.com/wcpe/USRodaleStore/pdf/football_physics/157954911XCHP.pdf+%22Tell+them+you+touched+it%22&hl=en&gl=us&ct=clnk&cd=1> (July 14, 2006).

4. "Rooney Gets His Wish," *The Super NFL,* January 12, 1975, <http://www.supernfl.com/SuperBowl/sb9.html> (July 14, 2006).

5. Ibid.

6. Chastain, p. 121.

7. "Super Bowl reflections: Terry Bradshaw," *Steelers.com,* n.d., <http://news.steelers.com/article/40516/> (July 17, 2006).

8. Dan Wetzel, "Super Bomb," *Yahoo! Sports,* February 1, 2005, <http://sports.yahoo.com/nfl/news?slug=dw-mitchell020105&prov=yhoo&type=lgns> (July 17, 2006).

9. "Super Bowl reflections: Terry Bradshaw."

10. Ibid.

11. "Those Same Old Steelers," *UK Black and Gold,* n.d., <http://www.pittsburghsteelers.co.uk/steelers/page7.htm> (July 18, 2006).

Chapter 4. The Power of Cowher

1. James Barger, ed., *Pittsburgh Post-Gazette, Decade of Power: The Pittsburgh Steelers in the Cowher Era* (Chicago: Triumph Books, 2002), p. 11.

2. Ibid., p. 43.

3. Associated Press, "Cowboys capture title despite Steelers' efforts," *Kansas State Collegian,* January 29, 1996, <http://www.kstatecollegian.com/ISSUES/v100/sp/n081/AP-Superbore.html> (July 20, 2006).

4. REI, "Heads or Tails," *Referee.com,* 2001, <http://www.referee.com/sampleArticles/2001/SampleArticle0101/headsortails/headstailstext.html> (March 2, 2007).

5. "NFL 2001," *Outsports.com,* n.d., <http://www.outsports.com/nfl/2001/championships.htm> (July 21, 2006).

6. Associated Press, "Steelers beat Browns on late rally," *NFL.com,* January 5, 2003, <http://www.nfl.com/gamecenter/recap/NFL_20030105_CLE@PIT> (July 21, 2006).

7. Associated Press, "Nedney boots Titans into AFC title game," *NFL.com,* January 11, 2003, <http://www.nfl.com/gamecenter/recap/NFL_20030111_PIT@TEN> (July 21, 2006).

8. Associated Press, "Ravens run past Steelers 30–13," *NFL.com,* September 19, 2004, <http://www.nfl.com/gamecenter/recap/NFL_20040919_PIT@BAL> (July 8, 2006).

9. "Steelers survive strange Colts rally, 21–18," *NFL.com,* January 15, 2006, <http://www.nfl.com/gamecenter/recap/NFL_20060115_PIT@IND> (July 8, 2006).

10. "Super Bowl XL," *nfluk.com,* n.d., <http://www.nfluk.com/news/news-latestresults.php> (July 9, 2006).

Chapter 5. The Masterminds

1. "Rooney Gets His Wish," *The Super NFL,* January 12, 1975, <http://www.supernfl.com/SuperBowl/sb9.html> (May 4, 2006).

2. "Arthur J. Rooney, 1901–1988," *UK Black and Gold,* n.d., <http://www.pittsburghsteelers.co.uk/steelers/rooneys/page1.htm> (May 5, 2006).

3. Bill Chastain, *Steel Dynasty: The Team That Changed the NFL* (Chicago: Triumph Books, 2005), p. 7.

Chapter Notes

4. "A Steelers' Tradition: 2000 Enshrinee Dan Rooney," *Official Site of the Pro Football Hall of Fame,* 2000, <http://www.profootballhof.com/hof/release.jsp?RELEASE_ID=719> (March 2, 2007).

5. Randy Roberts and David Welky (eds.), *The Steelers Reader* (Pittsburgh: University of Pittsburgh Press), 2001, pp. 136-137.

6. Ibid., p. 137.

7. Robert Dvorchak, "Steelers fans cope with reality," *post-gazette.com,* June 26, 2005, <http://www.post-gazette.com/pg/05177/528560.stm> (May 20, 2006).

8. Ed Bouchette, "On Solid Ground," *Football Digest,* August 2002, <http://www.findarticles.com/p/articles/mi_m0FCL/is_10_31/ai_86867348> (May 20, 2006).

Chapter 6. Welcome to Heinz Field

1. Myron Cope, "Towels & Points Delight," *Steelers Fever,* n.d., <http://www.steelersfever.com/terrible_towel.html> (July 2, 2006).

2. Ibid.

3. Doug Kennedy, "Hillgrove proud to be a 'homer,'" *PittsburghLive.com,* November 19, 2004, <http://www.pittsburghlive.com/x/pittsburghtrib/s_274334.html> (July 5, 2006).

Chapter 7. The Heroes

1. "'Whizzer' White career highlights," *dailycamera.com,* April 16, 2002, <http://www.thedailycamera.com/buffzone/sports/16swhiz.html> (June 2, 2006).

2. "Ernie Stautner Quotes," *CMG Worldwide,* n.d., <http://www.cmgworldwide.com/football/stautner/quote.html> (June 2, 2006).

3. Bill Chastain, *Steel Dynasty: The Team That Changed the NFL* (Chicago: Triumph Books, 2005), p. 25.

4. Chuck O'Donnell, "Jack Ham," *Football Digest,* December 2000, <http://www.findarticles.com/p/articles/mi_m0FCL/is_4_30/ai_66760545/pg_4> (June 4, 2006).

5. "PittsburghLive Community," *PittsburghLive.com,* n.d., <http://discuss.pittsburghlive.com/viewtopic.php?t=78628&postdays=0&postorder=asc&start=80&sid=582d2c0d8e61c7bb79010ae4f299ea47> (June 4, 2006).

6. Paul Zimmerman, "A Rose By Any Other Name," *Sports Illustrated,* July 30, 1984, <http://www.mcmillenandwife.com/lambert_man_of_steel.html> (June 8, 2006).

7. Ibid.

8. "Mel Blount," *SportingNews.com,* n.d., <http://archive.sportingnews.com/nfl/100/36.html> (June 6, 2006).

9. "Utterings By & About Terry Bradshaw," *McMillen and Wife's Pittsburgh Steelers,* n.d., <http://www.mcmillenandwife.com/bradshaw_quotes.html> (June 6, 2006).

10. "John Stallworth: Class of 2002," *Pro Football Hall of Fame,* n.d., <http://www.profootballhof.com/history/release.jsp?release_id=490> (June 10, 2006).

11. Merril Hoge, "Webster was a driven champion," *ESPN.com,* n.d., <http://espn.go.com/nfl/columns/hoge_merrill/1436020.html> (June 11, 2006).

12. Paul Attner, "Older but wiser," *The Sporting News,* September 28, 1998, <http://www.findarticles.com/p/articles/mi_m1208/is_n39_v222/ai_21174944/pg_2> (June 11, 2006).

13. Ibid.

14. Carl Prine, "Jerome Bettis, the NFL's King of Pain," *Pittsburgh Tribune-Review,* January 9, 2005, <http://www.pittsburghlive.com/x/pittsburghtrib/news/specialreports/specialnfl/s_291034.html> (June 13, 2006).

15. Paul Wiseman, "Ward spins biracial roots into blessing," *USA Today,* April 9, 2006, <http://www.usatoday.com/sports/football/nfl/steelers/2006-04-09-ward-focus_x.htm> (June 14, 2006).

16. Ibid.

Further Reading

Aikens, Jason and Mark Stewart. *The Pittsburgh Steelers.* Chicago: Norwood House Press, 2006.

Buckley Jr., James. *AFC North: The Baltimore Ravens, the Cincinnati Bengals, the Cleveland Browns, and the Pittsburgh Steelers.* Chanhassen, Minn.: Child's World, 2004.

———. *Super Bowl.* New York: DK Pub., 2003.

Frisch, Aaron. *Pittsburgh Steelers: Super Bowl Champions.* Mankato, Minn.: Creative Education, 2005.

Giglio, Joe. *Great Teams in Pro Football History.* Chicago, Ill.: Raintree, 2006.

Mendelson, Abby. *The Pittsburgh Steelers, 3rd Edition: The Official Team History.* Boulder, Colo.: Taylor Trade Publishing, 2006.

Pittsburgh Tribune-Review Staff, *Tough as Steel: Pittsburgh Steelers: 2006 Super Bowl Champions.* Greensburg, Pa.: Tribune-Review Publishing Company, 2006

Rappoport, Ken. *Super Sports Star Jerome Bettis.* Berkeley Heights, N.J.: Enslow Publishers, Inc., 2003.

Schmalzbauer, Adam. *The History of Pittsburgh Steelers: NFL Today.* Mankato, Minn.: Creative Education, 2004.

Wright, John. *Football.* Broomall, Penn.: Mason Crest Publishers, 2004.

Index

A
AFC Championship Game
- 1975–76 season, 34, 36
- 1984–85 season, 46
- 1992–93 season, 50
- 1994–95 season, 50–51
- 1995–96 season, 51
- 1997–98 season, 53
- 2001–02 season, 55–56
- 2003–04 season, 60
- 2005–06 season, 9, 62–63

AFC Divisional Playoff Games. *see* playoff games
Alexander, Shaun, *11,* 64
Allen, Jimmy, 30
Anderson, Gary, 50

B
Banaszak, John, 37
Bell, Kendrell, 55
Bettis, Jerome
- 2000–01 season, 54
- 2001–02 season, 55
- 2005–06 playoff games, 8–9, 60, 62
- acquired by Steelers, 53
- injuries, 7
- praised and celebrated, 9–10, 13
- profile, 110–111
- retirement, 7, 13
- Super Bowl, *6,* 10, 12–13

Bleier, Rocky, 31, 32–33, 36
Blount, Mel, 26, 34, 98–100, *99*
Bradshaw, Terry
- drafted by Steelers, 26
- MVP award, 37, 40–41, 44
- passes completed, 33–34
- playoff game, 1974, 31
- profile, 100, 101
- retirement, 45, *70*
- Super Bowls, *24, 101*

Brister, Bubby, 47
broadcasters, 74–76, 84–85, 86, 101
Burress, Plaxico, 55

C
Central Division Title. *see* division title wins
coaches
- Coach of the Year, 1992, 50
- Cowher, Bill, 49, 50, 76–77
- Noll, Chuck, 21–23, 44, 47, 71–74
- Parker, Ray, 18, 70–71
- Sutherland, Jock, 17–18

coal miners, 15
Cope, Myron, 73, 74–76, 84–85
Cowher, Bill, *48,* 49, 50, 76–77

D
Dallas Cowboys, 34–35, 37, 40–41, 51–52
defeats, trend of, 16, 18–19, 23, 46–47
Denver Broncos, 37
Detroit, 10
division title wins, 28–29, 37, 42
draft picks
- 1955, 18
- 1969, 22
- 1970, 25–26
- 1971, 26
- 1974, 30
- 1983, 45–46
- 2003, 58

Dungy, Tony, 37

E
Elway, John, 47

F
fan club, 87
Forbes Field, 16
Foster, Barry, 49, 50
Fuamatu-Ma'afala, Chris, 57
Furness, Steve, 37

Index

G
Greene, Kevin, 50
Greene, "Mean Joe," *38–39*
   drafted by Steelers, 22
   example to other players, 23
   Pro Bowl, 30
   profile, 92–93
   retirement, 45
Greenwood, L. C., 22, 30, *103*, 103–104
Guqua, John "Frenchy," 26

H
Haggans, Clark, 60
Hall of Fame (Pro Football)
   inductees, 30, 70, 95, 96, 100, 103, 106–108
Ham, Jack, 30, *42*, 45, 93–95
Harris, Franco, *95*
   1972–73 season, 27–28
   1974–75 playoffs, 31
   departure of, 45
   MVP award, 32
   profile, 95–96
   Super Bowl XIV, *24*
   yards ran, 1975 season, 34
Heinz Field, 55, *78*, 79–83
History of team.
   see also playoff games
   1930s–1950s, 15–18
   1960s, 18–23
   1970s, 26–44
   1980s, 44–47
   1990s, 47, 49–54
   2000–03, 54–58
   2004 season, 58–60
   2005 season, 60–65

I
"Immaculate Reception" play, 28–29, *95*
Indianapolis Colts, 61–62

J
journalists, 74, 86

K
Kansas City Chiefs, 50

Kids Club, Steelers, 87

L
Lambert, Jack, 30, 96, *97*, 98
Layne, Bobby, 71
locker room, *66*
Los Angeles Rams, 42–43

M
Maddox, Tommy, 56–57
Malone, Mark, 46
Marino, Dan, 46
Minnesota Vikings, 32
MVP award
   Bradshaw, Terry, 37, 41, 44
   Harris, Franco, 32
   Swann, Lynn, 102
   Ward, Hines, 113

N
National Football League
   franchise, *14*, 15
New England Patriots, 60
Noll, Chuck, *20*
   profile, 71–74
   respect of players toward, 26–27, 44
   retirement, 47
   selected as coach, 21–23
   training camp coaching, 33

O
Oakland Raiders, 28–30, 31, 36
O'Donnell, Neil, 50, 52–53, *54*
owners, team, 15, 67–70

P
Parker, Ray "Buddy," 18, 44, 70–71
Parker, Willie, 60, 64, *64*
Pittsburgh, 79–80
Pittsburgh Pirates, 16
playoff games
   1947, 17
   1972, 28–29
   1973–74 season, 29–30
   1974–75 season, 30–31

1976–77 season, 36
1977–78 season, 37
1979–80 season, 42
1982–83 season, 45
1984–85 season, 46
1989–90 season, 46–47
1993–94 season, 50
2002–03 season, 56–58
2003–04 season, 59
2005–06 season, 8–9, 60–62
Polamalu, Troy, 62
Porter, Joey, *11*, 60
Pro Bowl
  1975, 34
  1976, 36
  2001, 56

R

radio broadcasters, 74–76, 84–85, 86
Roethlisberger, Ben
  2004–05 season, 7
  2005–06 playoff games, 61, 61, 62
  draft selection, 58
  rookie records, 58–59
  Super Bowl, 10, 65
Rooney, Art, *14*, 15, 65, *66*, 67–69
Rooney, Art, III, *73*
Rooney, Dan, 69–70, *70*
Russell, Andy, 26, 30, 34

S

Seattle Seahawks, 12–13, 63–64
sportscasters, 74–76, 84–85, 86, 101
stadiums, home, 26, 54–55, 79–83
Stallworth, John, 30, 104–106, *105*
Stautner, Ernie, 90–91, *91*
steelworkers, 15

Stewart, Kordell, 53, 54, 55, 56
Sunday games, 15
Super Bowls
  1975 (IX), 31–32
  1976 (X), 34–36, *42*
  1979 (XIII), 37, 40–41, *101, 105*
  1980 (XIV), 24, 42–44
  1996 (XXX), 51–52
  2006 (XL), 10, *11*, 12–13, 63–65
  number of titles won, 12, 41, 44, 74
  records, 32, 41, 64
Sutherland, Jock, 17–18
Swann, Lynn, 24
  drafted by Steelers, 30
  playoff game, 1975, 31, *31*
  profile, 102–103
  retirement, 45
  Super Bowl XIV, 43
  touchdown receptions, 34

T

tailgating parties, 83–84
team names, 16–17
Terrible Towels, 84–85
Thigpen, Yancey, 51
Three Rivers Stadium, 26, 54, 79
Tomczak, Mike, 53, 54

U

Unitas, Johnny, 18

W

Ward, Hines, 55, 65, *112*, 113
Webster, Mike, 30, 106–108, *107*
White, Byron "Whizzer," *88*, 89–90
Williams, John L., 50
Woodson, Rod, 47, 50, 108–110, *109*

3/2 pg 13 damaged. jAj

BOCA RATON PUBLIC LIBRARY, FLORIDA
3 3656 0438488 3

J 796.33264 Are
Aretha, David
Steel tough--the Pittsburgh
Steelers

DISCARDED